HOUSEKEEPER UNDER THE MISTLETOE

HOUSEKEEPER UNDER THE MISTLETOE

BY

CARA COLTER

First published in Great Britain 2015
By Mills & Boon, an imprint of HarperCollins*Publishers*
1 London Bridge Street, London, SE1 9GF

Large Print edition 2016

© 2015 Cara Colter

ISBN: 978-0-263-26170-7

Our policy is to use papers that are natural, renewable and recyclable products and made from wood grown in sustainable forests. The logging and manufacturing processes conform to the legal environmental regulations of the country of origin.

Printed and bound in Great Britain
by CPI Antony Rowe, Chippenham, Wiltshire

To all the people who share my love
of the wild and untamed beauty
of Kootenay Lake.

CHAPTER ONE

"UNDER DIFFERENT CIRCUMSTANCES," Angelica Witherspoon muttered to herself, as she drove down a main street where the summer sun was filtered through a thick green canopy of leaves, "this is the kind of place I would adore."

The city of Nelson was nestled in the Selkirk mountain range of British Columbia. It was quaint and charming.

She angle parked her car and noted plenty of activity on the wide sidewalks in front of historical buildings. It made her feel safe enough to vacate her car and get out and stretch. Her muscles were cramped with tension. In the distance, she could catch glimpses of the sparkling waters of the west arm of Kootenay Lake.

Angie sighed with longing. "This is a place I would love to explore." But she reminded herself, sternly, it was her *old* life that would have allowed her to explore the vibrant, artsy and scenic community.

In her *new* life she was extraordinarily tired and on edge. And it took money to explore. Angie had six dollars and twenty-two cents left to her name. She had allowed herself one cash machine withdrawal and was still in shock at how quickly two hundred dollars, the maximum she could take, had evaporated.

Under a colorful awning, just in front of where she had parked her car, there was an outdoor café. The savory smells of rich coffee and of spicy Indian food enveloped her. She felt a pang of hunger. It was the first time in a week on the run that her stomach had unknotted enough for her to feel hungry.

But, she told herself, if she bought a loaf of bread, and some sliced meat she could make her six dollars and change go a bit further than if she gave in to the temptation to sit down to a restaurant meal. She looked around for a corner store.

Tires squealed off in the distance, a jarring

sound, and Angelica felt her heart begin to hammer, and a fine bead of sweat broke out on her lip. She fought terror as she scanned the street, making sure she was not being watched.

Inwardly, she talked herself down from the ledge.

"Of course you are not being watched," she chided herself. "How could anyone have followed you when you were not sure yourself where you were going?"

But it was part of this surplus of caution that wouldn't allow her to use the bank machine again. Winston had shown remarkable creativity in invading her life. What if he could track her transactions? No, she would find a loaf of bread. Peanut butter might be a better choice than meat, because it would be easier to keep.

And then what? she asked herself. With her quickly dwindling resources, she was going to have to give this up and go home?

Home. A shudder ran up and down her spine.

He'd been in her home, she reminded herself. Winston had been in her home. In her bedroom. What had he touched?

"Ugh," she said as repulsion shuddered down her spine, making her uncertain that she was ever going home again. But, realistically, she had to be back at school in September—summer would not last forever. Surely this would be over by then? What if it wasn't?

She thought of faces of her students, the changes she saw in those faces over one school year, the sense they gave her of being *needed*, and she nearly wept at the thought she might not be able to return to them and to the job she loved.

"Never mind that," she told herself firmly. That was all in the distant future. Right now there was a more urgent and immediate question. How was she going to get by for a few weeks until the police apprehended Winston?

"I just need a break," she whispered, heavenward. "One small break."

And that was when she noticed the community bulletin board. She was drawn to it as if it were a magnet and she a dropped pin. All else faded, and she saw only one posting.

In very masculine printing it read:

HOUSEKEEPER NEEDED IMMEDIATELY.
MATURE APPLICANTS ONLY.
EMPLOYER DESIRES QUIET AND PRI-
VACY.
CHATTERBOXES NEED NOT APPLY.
APPLY IN PERSON AT THE STONE
HOUSE, ANSLOW, BC.

Angelica snatched the scrap of paper down off the board like a starving pauper who had been tossed a crust. She glanced around surreptitiously, holding the paper close to her chest, as if others might be waiting to pounce on her and wrestle her to the ground for that job opportunity. It occurred to her she might be drawing attention to herself.

But Nelson seemed to be a place that embraced everything from the slightly eclectic to the downright weird, and no one was paying the slightest attention to her. She forced herself to relax and read the notice again, more slowly.

The position was probably long gone. There

was no date on it. The paper it was written on seemed frayed around the edges and slightly water damaged. On the other hand, it was downright unfriendly. Only someone desperate—that would be her—would be the slightest bit interested in such a posting.

She wasn't sure how "mature" would be defined, but considered herself a very mature twenty-five. She definitely was not a chatterbox, though she was outgoing and friendly, which was probably what had gotten her into trouble in the first place.

Angelica Witherspoon was being stalked.

Stalked. It was like something out of a movie. Three months ago, she had gone for one cup of coffee with someone she'd felt sorry for. Her life had been unraveling ever since.

Angelica forced herself to focus on the scrap of paper in her hand instead of revisiting what she could have done differently, where she went wrong.

She read it for the third time. In her mind, a picture formed of an elderly gentleman, sweetly crusty and curmudgeonly—maybe like the beautifully animated character in the movie *Up*—who found himself alone and needed some help around his house.

She had asked for one small break. And here it was. She had to grab it. Her resolve firmed within her. With her background in home economics, she was fully qualified for this job.

"Excuse me," she said. She was startled—and faintly ashamed—by how timid she sounded. It seemed that a minor annoyance deepening into something more sinister had changed everything about her in a very short amount of time.

The man going by her had dreadlocks and a multicolored striped knit toque despite the mid-July heat. He also looked as if he was wearing a skirt instead of pants. But when he stopped and looked at her, she saw he had friendly eyes.

"Where is Anslow?"

"Take the highway that way, around the lake. It's only fifty-eight kilometers, but it will take you an hour. The road is windy."

"Is there any other kind of road in British Columbia?" she asked wearily.

"Ah, an Albertan."

Just like that, without intending to, Angie had revealed things about herself, which Canadian province she lived in. If somebody was following her and came asking... Rationally, she knew the chances of this very same man being stopped and asked about her were slim to none, but her life was not rational, not right now.

"Saskatchewan, actually," she lied. She was aware the lie filled her with an odd sense of guilt, which she shook off. "Have you ever heard of the Stone House in Anslow?"

"No, but I like the possibilities."

Given his very Bohemian appearance and the faint, acrid smell of smoke coming from him, Angelica got his meaning and actually smiled. It was the first time she had smiled since coming home a week ago to find the campaign to infiltrate her life had escalated. The doors to her new apartment had still been locked, but a brand-new stuffed panda with a red bow around its neck had been residing jauntily against the pillows on her bed. She was sure her dresser drawers had been opened. This had been the final straw in a string of steadily escalating and upsetting incidents that had been going on for the three months since she had said an innocent yes to that cup of coffee.

The shock—finding the bear on her bed, the red ribbon looking horribly like a cut throat—had sent her pell-mell into flight mode. Still, after a week, it felt that no matter where she went, she wasn't far enough away yet.

Now, an hour and a half after leaving Nelson—she'd stopped to wolf down a peanut butter sandwich at a picnic area being enjoyed by several families—following instructions she had received in the town of Anslow, she pulled up to a formidable stone-pillared entrance that would not have looked out of place guarding the entrance to a haunted house. She hesitated but the wrought iron gate hung open, and really…? If she was looking for a place where it would be hard to find her, this was certainly it.

She could not see a house, just a long, deeply shaded drive that wound down to a sharp curve, where it disappeared.

She took the road slowly, around the curve, but still no house, just the drive, weaving its way through magnificent old-growth forest. Angelica opened her window, and birdsong and a wonderful smell, sun on fallen pine needles, wrapped around her.

She felt some of the edginess drain from her. It made the feeling of exhaustion intensify.

The road dropped down and down, drawing ever closer to the water. It wove its lazy way through the forest and occasionally broke out into cleared grasslands that allowed her to see the full and enormous expanse of Kootenay Lake. And then she would be back in the deep, cool shadows of the forest, catching only glimpses of the glinting waters of the lake.

Finally, after a good fifteen minutes of driving, the house came into view.

The name had led her to expect she would see a stone house. Instead, Angie saw it was possible the house was named for its location, anchored as it was into a slab of natural gray stone forty or fifty feet above the placid waters of the lake.

The gate and the picture of the curmudgeonly

little old man she had been working on had led her to expect a decrepit mansion.

Instead, the house before her was a masterpiece of modern architecture, blending with the elements around it. The house appeared to be constructed of 90 percent glass, the glass reflecting leaves and trees and sky at the same time as making the interior of the house and its contents seem as if it was an oasis that was magically suspended in the outdoors.

The huge expanse of windows made it possible to see right through the house, past a sectional white leather sofa and a stand-alone fireplace, to the deck on the other side of the dwelling. The deck, though huge, seemed to hold a single hammock, positioned in a way that took best advantage of the breathtaking view of the lake.

The setting and the house were stunningly beautiful. Angie imagined if you were inside the house it would feel as if nothing separated you from the forest on one side and the lake on the other.

It was not, to be sure, the house she would have expected a curmudgeonly old man to live in!

She suddenly felt ridiculously vulnerable. She was out here in the middle of nowhere, alone. No one, except the person she had asked for instructions in Anslow, knew she was here.

What if she was jumping from the frying pan into the fire?

"What are the chances," she asked herself, "that you could meet another deranged man in such a short span of time? None!"

Realistically, her situation—peanut butter and loaf of bread in the backseat not withstanding—couldn't be more desperate. The past three months had made her steadily more cowardly, but she had to call on what little courage remained in order to do what needed to be done.

She twisted her rearview mirror over and ran a hand through her hair, tried to tidy her blouse and straighten the crumples out of her shorts, which suddenly seemed too short. Despite her efforts, she could not lose the faintly disheveled look of a week of living out of a suitcase.

Then, putting her anxiety about her appearance aside, Angie parked her car under a towering pine. She got out and marched to the door of the house. Okay, she left the keys in the ignition and the door of her car open, just in case she had to make a quick getaway.

As she made the winding walk to the front door, she was aware again of a beautiful aroma, deep and woodsy, and a cacophony of birdsong.

It was a double-entry doorway and it was constructed of stainless steel, etched with a geometric pattern of interlocking squares. The leaves of the trees surrounding the house were casting dancing shadows on the surface. Despite the fact it needed a good scrubbing, it was more like a work of art than a door.

In the center was a ring of steel, and she grasped it firmly and rapped against the door. The sound was loud and pure, like a gong in a Buddhist temple, and it startled her. She was aware of the sound reverberating inside of her when the door swung inward soundlessly.

Angie was pretty sure her mouth had fallen before she snapped it shut.

The man who stood in front of her was about the furthest thing from a curmudgeon that she could imagine.

He was stunningly handsome.

He looked to be in his early thirties. Tall and powerfully built, he had brown hair, the exact color and sheen of a vat of melted dark chocolate. His hair was long enough to touch the collar of an untucked white denim shirt that needed pressing. His hair was faintly mussed, as if he had been out in the wind.

To add to the pirate-straight-off-the-boat look of him, his cheekbones and chin were cast in the dark shadows of a day or two of whisker growth. His legs were long and set apart, braced, which showed the powerful cut of his thigh muscles underneath the faded denim of blue jeans. His feet were bare, which Angie was perturbed to note she found sexy. She hastily lifted her eyes from them to look him in the face.

His eyes were astonishing, the same restless gray blue of the waters of the lake she could see through wall-to-wall windows beyond him. But the water looked welcoming on this sweltering day, and nothing about his expression, and especially not his eyes, welcomed. And still, his eyes were every bit as sexy as his bare feet had been!

He regarded her with a furrowed brow for a moment, the line of his sensuous mouth pulled down in a surprised frown.

"Nope," he said. It was a single word. Despite the fact his voice was a rasp of pure unwelcome, there was something about it that made Angelica even more aware of what an almost criminally attractive man he was, blatantly sexy without even trying.

Apparently, the attraction was not shared. He shut the door. It clicked closed with metallic finality.

CHAPTER TWO

"Nope."

The gravelly rejection rang in Angie's ears for long moments after the door had clicked shut.

Oddly, her first reaction to the door being slammed in her face was relief. She reminded herself she no longer wanted men to find her attractive. It was dangerous. Plus, if he was deranged, he could have taken advantage of the isolation to pull her inside that house. Instead, he was dismissing her.

Though, looking into the strong cast of his face, the intelligence in his eyes, the confidence of his bearing, derangement did not seem like even a remote possibility.

She recognized her relief at the closing of the door, in part, not just because he was obviously not a pervert just waiting for a damsel in distress to land at his door, but because she had reacted to him in a very primal way, and she could not tolerate that in herself.

In the past year her fiancé, Harry, had abandoned her in favor of a beach in Thailand, and a more exciting companion, and now she was being stalked by a maniac. If anyone should be absolutely immune to the charms of the opposite sex, it was her! But apparently she wasn't. So, she should be glad of that door closed with such quiet finality.

But she wasn't. In fact, the relief that she was being dismissed was short-lived, indeed. It gave way to a stirring of indignation at his summary dismissal. And indignation felt so much better than the wound she had carried with her since Harry had shattered her dreams.

And it felt *way* better than the cowering scared-of-her-own-shadow fear she had been living with ever since Winston's escalating invasion of her life.

Angie decided, right that second, that she was not going to be a victim anymore.

Besides, she *needed* this position as a housekeeper. It was an answer to that whispered prayer she had said at the bulletin board in Nelson just a few hours ago.

Angelica took a deep breath. She marshaled her courage. She set her chin and her shoulders. And then she lifted that ring of steel again and rapped it against his door with all the gumption she could muster.

"Damn him," she muttered, when it seemed the master of the Stone House intended to ignore her. She drew in a sharp breath, marshalled her threads of tattered courage, and then she grasped the ring again.

Her hand was clutching the door knocker with the fierce determination of a drowning person clutching a life ring when the door was yanked open.

The unexpected force pulled Angie over the threshold and into the cool, marbled foyer of his house. She stumbled, let go of the knocker—a full second too late—and put out her hands to stop her forward momentum.

Angie's hands ran straight into a solid wall... of man.

She stared at her hands on his chest. Through

the fabric of his shirt she could feel the steady, slow beat of his heart and the shocking heat of his skin. She could feel the utter and steely power of him. His scent was masculine, absolutely tantalizing and utterly spellbinding. He smelled of sunshine and lake water and pine trees. Angie dragged her gaze away from the wide expanse of manly and mesmerizing chest in front of her.

Those gorgeous stormy-water eyes were fastened, with some consternation, on the placement of her hands, which for some reason she had not yet removed from his person!

She gulped, came out of her trance, and snapped her hands off his chest and down to her sides. She took a giant step backward.

He raised his eyes from where her hands had been glued to him and tilted his head at her. "You're still here," he said.

His tone was laconic, but his eyes were narrowed with annoyance. There was a little muscle flicking in the uncompromising line of his unshaven jaw. It was fascinating.

"Um," she said intelligently.

"Yes?"

"I just needed to know."

"Know?"

"*Nope* to what?" Angie was trying very hard to regain her sense of equilibrium. She reminded herself to straighten her shoulders and lift her chin.

He seemed surprised that she would have the audacity to even question him. He regarded her piercingly.

"I mean, who answers their door like that? With a single word? Nope? When you don't even know why I'm here." Angie had to remind herself of her vow not to be a victim anymore. Still, she had to fight herself not to fidget, to hold her chin firmly in place and her shoulders square. He regarded her silently, with lowered brows and narrowed eyes. She was certain that he intended to let her stew, to see if he could make her squirm. She held her ground.

Finally, he sighed. The sound was one of pure exasperation, and yet she felt certain his expelled breath had touched her cheek, like a kiss. It was everything she could do to keep her hands at her sides and not touch her cheek.

"Nope to whatever you're selling." His voice was stern and annoyed, not the voice of a man who could kiss cheeks with his very breath.

"But you don't even know what I'm selling!" she protested. Was that a quaver in her voice?

"Yes, I do." His voice was like gravel.

"You don't," she said stubbornly.

"I do."

I do. The words she had expected to be hearing from Harry. Even said out of context, they filled Angie with a longing that made her despise herself. How many kicks in the teeth did a gal have to endure before she got it? There was no knight in shining armor. There was no happily ever after. Those kind of illusions were what got people in trouble.

"Girl Guide cookies," he said, his voice hard, "or your version of enlightenment, or tickets to the high school play. And to all of those, an emphatic nope."

See? This man was the cynical type. He would never fall victim to illusions of any kind.

"As a matter of fact," she said, stripping any trace of quaver—or illusions—from her voice, "you're wrong on all counts. I am not selling anything."

This man was not accustomed to being told he was wrong. She could see that instantly, when the dark slashes of his brows dropped dangerously.

Angie told herself she needed to be careful not to be off-putting. He was going to be her future boss, after all!

"I've come about your posting on the community board in Nelson," she told him.

The firm line of his lips deepened into a frown. That, coupled with his lowered brows, made it inarguable. Her future boss was scowling at her. He had no idea what she was talking about.

"I'm here about the position you advertised for a housekeeper."

His eyebrows shot up. His gaze swept her. "Oh," he said, "that."

"Yes, that."

He gave her another long look, apparently

contemplating her suitability for the position. She tried for her most housekeeperly expression.

"Especially nope to that," he said.

When the door began to whisper shut, again, it was pure desperation that made Angie put one foot in to stop it.

The man—good God, was he Heathcliff from Wuthering Heights—glanced down at her foot with astonished irritation. And then he gave her a look so icily reserved it should have made her withdraw her foot and touch her forelock immediately. But it did not. Angie held her ground.

The master of the mansion glared back down at her foot with deep annoyance, but she refused to retreat. She couldn't!

After a moment, he sighed again, and once more she felt the sensuous heat of his breath whisper across her cheek.

Then he opened the door wide and leaned the breadth of one of those amazing shoulders against the jamb, the seeming casualness of his stance not fooling her. Every fiber of his being was practically vibrating with displeasure. He folded his arms over the immenseness of his chest and tilted his head at her, waiting for an explanation for her audacity.

Really, all that icy remoteness should not have made him *more* attractive. But the impatient frown tugging at the edges of those too-stern lips made her think renegade thoughts of what was beyond the ice and what it would be like to know that.

These were crazy thoughts. This man was making her think crazy thoughts. She was a woman who had suffered so completely at the hands of love.

First, her Harry had decided all their dreams together were decidedly stodgy and had replaced her with insulting quickness with someone far more exotic and exciting.

And then, a coworker, Winston, had taken total advantage of her brokenhearted vulnerability. She had caved to his constant requests. Angie had said yes instead of no to a single cup of coffee. He had used that yes to force his way into her life.

With that kind of track record, it made her thoroughly annoyed with herself for even noticing what the master of the Stone House looked like. And what his voice sounded like. And what he smelled like. And what his breath had felt like grazing the tenderness of her cheek.

If she had a choice, she would have cut and run. But she was desperate. She had absolutely no choice.

With her foot against the door he was too polite to slam, she said, determined, "I need this job."

He contemplated that, and her, in silence.

"Really," she clarified when it seemed as if he was not going to say anything at all.

"Well, you don't qualify." His determination seemed to match her own. Or exceed it.

"In what way?"

"You're obviously not mature."

"I guess that would depend how you defined mature," she said.

"Old."

"How old?" she pressed. "Fifty? Sixty? Seventy? Eighty?" She hoped she was pointing out how ridiculous he was being. *Old* was not necessarily a great qualification in a housekeeper.

For a moment he said nothing, and then one corner of that sinfully sexy mouth lifted, but not in a nice way. "Older than you."

"I'm sure the human rights commission would have quite a bit to say about not being considered for a job—for which I'm perfectly qualified—because of my age," she said.

The smile deepened, tickling across his lips—cool, unfriendly, dangerous—and then he doused it and lowered the slash of his brows at her. "Are you threatening me?"

It occurred to her that annoying him would be the worst possible way to wiggle her way into this job position.

"No, not at all. I'm just suggesting that you might have attracted a better response to your posting for an available position if you had said you needed someone highly organized and hardworking and honest."

"All of which I'm presuming you are?" he said drily.

She took it as very hopeful that he had not tried to physically shove her foot out the door and slam it on her.

Not that he looked like a man who ever had to get physical to get what he wanted. That look he was giving her was daunting. Anyone less desperate would have backed down long before now.

"I'm desperate." There she had admitted it to him.

"Your desperation is not my con—"

"I'm willing to guess you haven't had a single response to that ad," she plowed on. "Who would answer an ad like that?"

"Apparently, you would."

"I'm not *just* desperate."

"How very nice for you," he said, his tone so sardonic it had a knife's edge to it.

"I'm also highly organized and hardworking and honest."

"You're too young."

"Humph. I think youth could be a great advantage for this position."

He didn't answer, so she rushed on.

"I will be terrific at this job. You'll love me."

He looked insultingly dubious about that.

How could she have said that? That he would

love her? You did not want to even think a word like that in front of a man like this—who could make you feel as if he had kissed you by simply sighing in your direction.

"I'll work for free for one day. If you're not impressed, you haven't lost anything."

He frowned at her. "Look, Miss—"

"Nelson," she filled in, using the name of the town she had just come through. "Brook Nelson." There. A new name. She had used part of the city of Cranbrook that she had passed through on this wild ride, and part of the town of Nelson.

She held her breath, knowing from the tension she felt while she waited that she *needed* the new existence her new name promised her.

CHAPTER THREE

JEFFERSON STONE REGARDED his unwanted visitor. Something shivered along his spine when she said her name. He knew she was lying.

And she wasn't very good at lying, either. In fact, she was terrible at it.

He allowed himself to study her more closely. Brook Nelson—or whoever the hell she really was—was cute as a button. She was dressed in a brightly patterned summer blouse and white shorts. She was a little bit of a thing, slender and not very tall. It looked as if a good wind would pick her up and toss her.

And yet when her hands had been pressed into his chest, he had been aware of something substantial about her. That little bit of a thing had set off a tingle in him—an awareness—that had been as unwelcome as she was.

Hard not to be aware of her, when those shorts

ended midthigh and showed off quite a bit of her legs.

Annoyed with himself, Jefferson shook off the thought and continued his study of his house-keeper candidate.

It just underscored what he already knew: she would not do.

She had light hair, a few shades darker than blond, but not brown. Golden, like sand he had seen on Kaiteriteri Beach in New Zealand. That hair was cut short, he suspected in a largely unsuccessful effort to make those plump curls behave themselves. They weren't. They were corkscrewing around her head in a most un-ruly manner.

Her eyes were hazel, leaning toward the gold side of that autumn-like combination of golds and greens and browns. She had delicate fea-tures and it was probably that scattering of freckles across her nose that made her seem so wholesome, even though she was lying about who she was.

There was something earnest about her. De-spite her youth, and despite the shortness of those shorts, she seemed faintly prim, as if she would be easily shocked by bad words. Which, of course, was part of the reason she would be a very bad fit for him as a housekeeper.

Because of her size, Jefferson had assumed she was young. But on closer inspection, she looked as if she was in her midtwenties. Still, she was exactly the type you would expect to be peddling cookies for a good cause or wanting to change the world for the better or encouraging attendance at the annual Anslow high school performance of *Grease*, which would be dreadful.

And he should know. Because a long time ago, in a different life, he had been cast as the renegade in that very high school play.

Jefferson shook it off. He did not like reminders of his past life.

Besides, Brook wasn't anything like the ideal person he had in his head for this job, which was gray haired, motherly but not chatty, and someone willing to stay out of his way and keep schtum about his life.

Brook Nelson, in spite of the wholesome exterior and her claims of honesty, was lying about who she was. He needed her gone.

"Look, Miss, um, Nelson, I've gone through three housekeepers in three weeks—"

"Somebody answered *that* ad?" she asked disbelievingly.

"Not exactly," he had to admit. "*That* ad was a result of the other failures."

The failure was that he had mentioned to Maggie, at the Anslow Emporium, that he was going to need someone.

He hadn't anticipated that telling Maggie—whom he had known since he was six—that he needed some help at his house would be like creating a posting in a lonely hearts club rag.

"Tell me about my three predecessors."

He frowned at that. She was a cheeky little thing, wasn't she? What part of no could she not get? But, since she was immune to slamming doors, why not give her anecdotal evidence of her unsuitability for this position?

"Okay, the first one was *not* mature. Mandy, showed up in flip-flops, and had a most irritating way of popping her gum, except when she was texting on her cell phone, which seemed to require her jaw to stop moving. When she had been here approximately three hours, she knocked on my office door to complain that the internet signal was weak from the deck. And then she acted insulted when I suggested I didn't need her services any longer."

Jefferson did not mention that Mandy had told him that she was prepared to overlook the vast difference in their ages if he wanted to give it a try.

He had escorted her to the door with a sense of urgency almost unparalleled in his life—and before finding out exactly what "it" meant.

"The second one was also not *mature.* She had on too much mascara and her skirt was too short, and she seemed way too interested—"

He stopped.

"In you?" Brook asked quietly.

He didn't want to get into that. He was a small-town boy who had left here, made good of himself and then come home with a wife. He should have figured out, before he took his request to Maggie, that now that Hailey had been dead over three years, he would be perceived, by the good and simple people of his hometown, as a rather tragic figure. Which was nothing new. He'd come to live with his grandparents when he was six, after his parents had died. He sometimes wondered why he had come back here, to this place where he had been and always would be the little orphan.

And now a widower, seen by one and all as much more in need of a new wife than a housekeeper.

"You don't have to worry about that with me," Brook piped up. "I have no romantic inclinations at all. None."

Brook seemed too young to have developed a truly jaundiced attitude toward romance, and Jefferson remembered housekeeper number two's rather frightening avarice.

He focused on her work performance flaws instead of telling Brook the full truth. "She also said *youse* instead of you. *Do youse want the toilet seat left up or down?*"

"You don't have to worry about that with me, either," Brook rushed to assure him. "There are few things I love as much as the English language and its correct usage."

"Hmm. That is not adding up to housekeeper, really. A true housekeeper might have been more concerned about the toilet seat and its correct usage."

A delicate blush crept up her cheeks.

"I'm a student," she said, "desperate for a summer job."

The desperate part was true enough, he could see that. But her eyes had done a slow slide to the right when she had said she was a student.

"My third housekeeper was Clementine." Clementine had been sent after he'd gone back down to the Emporium and read Maggie the riot act.

"She was certainly more suitable in the mature department. She'd actually been a friend of my grandmother's. But Clementine started talking the second she got in the door and did not stop, ever."

Jefferson remembered how even the lock on his office had not stopped her. "She stood outside my office while mopping the floor and polishing the door handle, chattering about her Sam. Husband. Mickey and Dorian. Children. Sylvester and Tweety. Bird and cat."

Suddenly it occurred to Jefferson, he *was* being the chatty one. This stranger standing at his door—whom he had absolutely no intention of hiring—certainly did not need all of this information.

Maybe it was a sign of too much time alone— three failed housekeepers not withstanding— that he just kept talking.

"I barricaded myself inside my office for three days, but Clem showed no sign of moving on to other parts of the house. To avoid discussion, I finally shot a generous check and a nice note about how I really didn't need her anymore under the door. It achieved exactly what I hoped—blessed silence."

He had managed to stop talking before he revealed Clementine's real fatal flaw. She had one divorced stepdaughter and three single nieces, all of whom she thought he should meet.

Brook's lips twitched. That hint of a smile deepened Jefferson's awareness of her as what he wanted least in his house: the distraction of an attractive woman. But that tentative smile also made him aware of the fine lines of tension in her—around her shoulders and neck, around her eyes, around her lips.

"It must have been hard to fire a friend of your grandmother's."

"You have no idea," he said.

But, looking at her, he had the uneasy feeling she *did* have an idea.

"Why the sudden search for a housekeeper? Are you replacing a housekeeper you were quite satisfied with?"

He scowled at her. Who was interviewing whom, here?

"No, I've never felt the need of one before."

"And now?"

He sighed. "In a moment of weakness, I agreed to allow an architectural magazine to photograph the house."

She glanced past him. "A moment of weakness? The house is extraordinary. You must be very honored at their interest."

"I may have been when it was all just an idea.

But as soon as a date was set, I realized the house would need attention, which, six weeks later, I am no closer to giving it."

"When is the photo session scheduled?"

"Two weeks." He was aware he was engaging with her, and it didn't seem to be bringing him any closer to getting rid of her.

"I can have your place completely ready for a photo shoot in two weeks. I promise."

Jefferson contemplated that. It was a weakness to contemplate it. But he did need someone to get the place ready, and the date of the photo shoot was creeping up far more rapidly than he could have believed. And he suspected, from the lack of applicants now, that word had spread far and wide through this tight-knit region of the Kootenays that he was impossible to work for.

So, the young woman in front of him could be considered a godsend, if one was inclined to think that way, which Jefferson Stone most definitely was not.

No, Nelson Brook, or Brook Nelson, or whatever her name was, just wasn't going to work out, despite the fact no one else had responded to his blunt posting that had laid out exactly what he needed. He would just have to postpone *Architecture Now* indefinitely. He was aware of feeling relieved at that possibility.

He reached for the door. He was going to gently shove on it until she moved her foot.

But then a crow cawed loudly and raucously in the tree the prospective housekeeper had parked her car under. It dropped a pinecone out of its beak onto the roof of her car, and both sounds, the cawing and the sharp plunk of the cone on her car roof, were loud and unexpected in the drowsy quiet of the afternoon.

She gasped and jumped forward, and she smashed against him. For the second time, in the space of just a few minutes, she was touching him.

Only this time, it wasn't her hands splayed across his chest, which had been disconcerting enough. This time he could feel the press of the entire length of her body against his, and he was acutely aware of the sweet softness of her. He was acutely aware of hesitating a fraction of a second too long before putting her away from him.

"I'm so sorry," she stammered, but he caught the look on her face as she swiveled her head and glanced over her shoulder. It was the frantic look of a deer being startled by wolves. When she turned back to him, despite the fact she was trying hard to school her features, he could see the pulse pounding in the hollow of her throat.

Tension trembled in the air around her, and her muscles had gone taut. It made him notice there were shadows under her eyes and an edginess about her that was far from normal.

Her car door, he noticed, looking beyond her, was open, as if she had planned what to do if she needed to make a quick getaway.

Brook Nelson, or whoever she was, was terrified of something.

What shocked Jefferson was how her fear pierced the armor around his heart. It was as if a little sliver of light found its way to a place that had been in total darkness.

Inside himself was some nearly forgotten sense of decency, some sense of being connected to a human family he'd managed to ignore for three whole years, much to the dismay of the people of Anslow.

Jefferson stood very still. For a moment, he thought of the grandparents who had raised him, in a house not far from here. They had been old-fashioned people, who were decent to the core and kind to a fault. They would have never turned someone in need from their door, and no one had benefited from their generosity of spirit more than him. He could almost imagine the look of disapproval on both their faces if he shut the door now.

Jefferson took a deep breath and looked into the pleading eyes of the woman who had landed, uninvited, on his doorstep.

Was this who he had become? So embittered by the death of his wife, Hailey, that he could turn a woman, so obviously terrified, away from his door?

"Jeez," Jefferson muttered under his breath. He was a man who made decisions every day. That was what he did for a living. The decisions he made altered the courses of entire cities, impacted huge companies and global corporations. His decisions often had millions of dollars and the livelihoods of thousands of people riding on them.

And yet, this decision, this split-second decision, about what kind of man he would be, felt bigger than all of those.

Jefferson Stone stepped back marginally from his door.

It was all Brook Nelson needed. She catapulted over his threshold and into his house.

Into his life, he told himself grimly.

"Thank you," she breathed.

"Nothing has been decided," he told her gruffly, though somehow he knew it had been. And she knew it, too. She was beaming at him.

"It's not going to be a walk in the park," he said. He was already annoyed that his decision had been based on a moment of pure emotion, not rationale. He had to get things back on track and make sure she was aware this was a professional arrangement. "The finer aspects of housekeeping have been neglected for a long time."

He fully intended to tell her that if she didn't

put them right he would not tolerate her presence any longer than he had her predecessors. But she spoke before he could get the grim warning out.

"I could tell that from this door that things have been slightly neglected," she said, tapping the front door. "It needs polishing. You probably use something special for it, do you?"

"I have no idea. That's your job, not mine." He was trying to make up for his moment of weakness in letting her in, but she didn't seem to notice uninviting his tone.

"Do you have an internet connection here?"

"Not one that housekeeper number one, Mandy, approved of, but my career is dependent on being connected."

"I'll just look up online what to use on a door like that one. Is it stainless steel, like kitchen appliances?"

He considered her question. She was focusing on the job at hand and not asking any personal questions about his career. Hopefully, that indicated a lack of nosiness. Hopefully, that indicated his impulsive decision to let her in was not going to lead to complete disaster. "Yes."

"I know I just use a few drops of vegetable oil on mine. At home."

So, there was a home, somewhere, and presumably a fairly nice one if it had stainless steel appliances in it.

Despite his intention to keep everything professional, he smelled man problems in his new housekeeper's personal life. She had already claimed she had no romantic notions, which basically meant *burned by love.* It would be nothing but good for him if she was sour on the whole relationship thing. It could be almost as good protection as *mature* and *silent.* And, despite the fact he had his own history that had turned his heart to the same stone as his name, he sensed a need to keep up his defenses and to demonstrate the same lack of nosiness that she was showing!

Still, she wasn't just having man problems. She was terrified.

CHAPTER FOUR

JEFFERSON CONTEMPLATED HOW Brook's obvious terror stirred an emotion in him that he did not feel ready to identify and, in fact, felt a need to distance himself from.

He'd been living—despite the efforts of the townspeople—without the complication of untidy emotions for some time.

He'd give this woman—Brook Nelson, or whoever she was—a break. That didn't mean he had to involve himself in her drama in any way. The house was ridiculously large. With the slightest effort, during the day he wouldn't even know she was here.

Though that might pose some challenges, because she was in his living room now, and despite the fact the windows let in all kinds of light, it was as if sunshine had poured into the room with her. She flounced into his living room, hands on her hips, eyes narrowed, lips pursed.

"Wow," she said.

He thought she was referring to the architecture, which generally inspired awe, but she turned disapproving eyes to him. "Good grief, I can see neither Mandy nor Clementine got to this room. You mustn't have allergies. How long since this has been dusted?"

"A while," he admitted, instead of *never*.

"And I take it, it would have gone a while longer if it weren't for the photo shoot?"

"That's correct."

"You are a true bachelor, aren't you? Why live in such a beautiful house if you aren't going to take care of it?" she wailed with genuine frustration.

"I'm a widower," he said tersely.

He was not sure why he had imparted that little piece of information. He hoped it wasn't because he thought that would make her more sympathetic to his slovenliness than being a bachelor would.

But, as soon as he saw the sympathy blaze in

her eyes, he realized he did not want her sympathy. Arriving in Anslow as an orphan, losing his wife, Jefferson Stone had experienced enough sympathy to last him a lifetime. He did not want any more challenges to his armor. He realized he needed to be much more vigilant in his separation of the professional and personal.

"I'm sorry," she said, her voice a low whisper that could make a man long for a bit of softness in his life.

But he had had softness, Jefferson reminded himself, and had proved himself entirely unworthy of it.

He lifted a shoulder in defense against the sympathy that blazed in her eyes. "My wife was the architect who designed the house."

"Ah, that explains a lot."

He lifted an eyebrow at her.

"You don't really seem like the type of person who would be amenable to having your home photographed. You are honoring her. That's nice."

Jefferson really didn't want her to think he was nice, and he squinted dangerously at her.

She got the message, because she moved over to an enlarged black-and-white photo on the wall.

"Who is this?"

The people responsible for the fact you haven't been sent packing. "It's me, with my grandparents, in front of the old house."

"It's a very powerful photograph."

That's what Hailey had said, too. She wasn't into hanging family portraits, but she had unearthed this photo and had it enlarged to four feet by six feet and transferred to canvas.

"How old are you in it?"

"Six."

She turned and looked at him. "How come you look so sad?" she asked.

He started. Hailey had never asked a single question about the photo. She had considered it an art piece. She had liked the composition, the logs of the old house, the dog on the porch, the hayfork leaning against the railing.

This woman was looking at him as if all his losses were being laid out before her, and he hated it.

"My parents had just died." He kept his tone crisp, not inviting any comment, but he saw the stricken look on her face before she turned away from him and ran her finger along the bottom of the frame.

She looked at her finger but didn't say anything. Her expression said it all. She felt sorry for him. No, it was more than sorry. She was, he could tell, despite the lie about her name, the softhearted type. She didn't just feel sorry for him. Her heart was breaking for him. And he hated that.

"This is a temporary position," he said, his voice cold. "After the photo shoot, I'll return to companionship of my dust bunnies. Maybe you want to consider if two weeks employment is what you are really looking for."

It was a last-ditch effort to let her know this position probably was not going to work for her. Or him.

"Temporary works perfectly for me," she said, as if that made it cosmically ordained. "Two weeks. I have a lot to do."

She had been careful not to express sympathy, and yet Jefferson felt her *I have a lot to do* could somehow mean rescuing him. Just a second. Wasn't he rescuing her? And if she thought she was going to turn the tables on him, she was in for an ugly surprise.

"We haven't come to terms yet. What do you expect for remuneration?"

"I haven't passed the free-day test yet."

He looked at her face. The softness lingered, but he was willing to bet she was one of those overachiever types. He deduced if she set out to impress, he would be impressed.

"Let's assume," he said drily.

She named a figure that seemed criminally low. But then she added, "Plus room and board, of course."

Jefferson stared at her. Why was this coming as a surprise to him? Obviously, some fear had sent her down his driveway, and just as obviously she was not eager to go back to it.

"I'm in the middle of relocating," Brook said vaguely. Then, as if sensing how disconcerted he was, she added, "This looks like a huge place. There must be a spare bedroom? Or two? Or a dozen?"

"I'm not sure—"

"Besides, if I'm going to be a proper house-keeper, I should probably make you some meals. That would be easier to do in residence, don't you think?"

He saw it again. Behind her I'm-going-to-be-the-best-housekeeper-in-the-world bravado was terror.

She *wanted* to stay here.

Under his roof and his protection. He supposed if you were looking for a place to hide, the Stone House fit the bill quite nicely, as long as the things you were hiding from were outside of yourself.

Jefferson wondered if his new housekeeper would feel quite so eager to seek shelter here if she knew how colossally he had failed the one other woman, his wife, who had expected protection from him.

Meals. He hadn't really even considered a housekeeper providing meals. His search for a housekeeper had been motivated strictly by getting the house ready for the magazine photo shoot. He considered telling her meals would not be part of their agreement but found himself oddly reluctant to do so. He had not had a home-cooked meal in longer than he could remember, and his mouth was watering. His weakness annoyed him.

"Look," he told Brook sternly. "Against my better judgment, I'm giving you a chance, but be warned, if you chatter, you're out of here."

She looked as if she might say something. But then she pursed her lips, brought her fingers up, locked and put the imaginary key in her pocket. But before he could even be properly relieved, she reached into that imaginary pocket, took out the key and unlocked her lips.

"Maybe just before we begin our vow of silence, I should get you to show me around and you can tell me what you'd like to see prioritized. I'll make a list of what each room needs."

It was a reasonable request, and he knew he could not really refuse it.

"Let's begin here," she coaxed, when he was silent.

"This room is the great room," he said. "I noticed the windows are rain spotted."

"The windows would be a priority," she agreed. "But I should probably leave them until right before the photo shoot so they just sparkle that day, right?"

"Right," he said, though of course he had not thought of that.

"Dusting." She looked up at the high vault of the ceiling. "You have a ladder somewhere? I see cobwebs up there."

He frowned up at where she was looking. He did not like spiders. Before he answered, she went and slapped the couch, and a cloud of dust flew up from it. "Vacuuming. If the weather stays nice, I might even put the furniture outside for a bit to air it out."

He couldn't really imagine she was going to get all that furniture outside by herself. The sectional was huge. And apparently she was going to need a ladder. Actually, he was not going to let her up on a ladder, so there was no point in finding one. He needed to make it clear he was not going to be roped into interaction with her. He was going to protest, but then she went on.

"It smells faintly stale in here. I think a good airing of the furniture will change that."

It smelled stale in his house?

"For the photo shoot," she said, a little pensively, "it might be nice to make it look lived in. You don't use this room much, do you?"

"Not really." She was proving to be uncomfortably astute.

"What would you think if we set it up a bit?" *We?*

"We could just add a bit of color. Maybe a bright throw over the couch, a few glossy magazines on display, a vase of flowers."

"Don't you think the photographer will do that?"

"Well, if he doesn't think to bring a vase of flowers with him, you'd be out of luck, since the nearest vase of fresh flowers would be quite a distance away. I could make the throw. I'll snoop around and see what you have."

He must have looked unconvinced because she rushed on, "You'd be surprised what you can make things out of. And I'm pretty handy with a needle and thread. I made this blouse."

That made him stare at the blouse for an uncomfortable second.

Thankfully, she had moved on. "It's just that this room—the house—is so beautiful, but it doesn't look very homey. It would make me happy to help it look its very best."

He stared at her. She already appeared much happier than she had when she first arrived, that little furrow of worry easing on her brow.

"I'll leave it up to you to spruce it up however you see fit. If you need to buy a few things, let me know," he said, and was annoyed that he felt he was giving in to her in some subtle but irreversible way. "Stay out of my office. And my bedroom."

The fact that he did not want her in his bedroom, that most intimate of spaces, alerted him to the fact she—this little mite of a woman in her homemade blouse with her wayward curls—was threatening him in some way that he had not allowed himself to be threatened in, in a very long time. If ever.

"But surely they'll want to photograph those rooms, too?"

"I'm quite capable of getting two rooms ready." His tone was curt and did not invite any more discussion, but he was aware that she had to bite her lip to keep herself from discussing it.

"I'll show you the kitchen," he said stiffly, leading her through to that room.

"Whoa," she said, following him, "now *this* is a room you use."

She didn't say it as if it was a good thing.

He looked at the kitchen through her eyes. The sink was full of dishes. She didn't know yet, but so was the oven. His mail was sliding off the kitchen table, and there were several envelopes on the floor. The counter by the coffeemaker was littered with grounds and sticky spoons. He often tromped up from the beach, wet, across the deck and through the kitchen. His bare footprints were outlined against the dark hardwood of a floor he'd allowed to become distinctly grimy.

Instead of looking daunted by the mess, she

gave him a smile. "You need me way more than you thought you did."

He looked at her. In this room, as in the living room, it felt as if her presence had made the light come on.

He had the terrible feeling that maybe he did need her more than he had thought he did. His life had become a gray wash of work and isolation.

And damn it, he told himself, *he liked it that way.* What he didn't like was that Brook had been in his domain for only a few minutes, and he already was seeing things about himself that he had managed to avoid for a long, long time.

"Look, I have work to do," he said. "I'm going to let you poke around the rest of the place by yourself. I'm sure it will become very quickly apparent to you what needs to be done."

He could have left then, but he watched as she wandered over to where the mail had fallen on the floor.

"This one is marked Urgent," she said. She came across the distance that separated them and held out the envelope. He reached for it.

For just a moment, their hands brushed. Something tingled along his spine, an electrical awareness of her. She might have felt something, too, because she spun away from him and went to the kitchen counter. It had a long, sleek window that overlooked the lake. But she did not look out the window. She opened up a cupboard.

"Is this what you're eating?" she asked him, holding up a soup can, and then setting that down and holding up a stew can.

He folded his arms over his chest, uninviting.

She ignored that. "Canned food is very high in sodium," she told him. "At your age, you have to watch things like that."

"My age?" he sputtered.

And then she laughed. It was a tinkling sound, as refreshing as a brook finding its way over pebbles.

"Do you have any fresh food?"

"Not really. There might be a few things in the freezer."

"That's not fresh. What do you eat?"

He thought of the stacks of microwavable

meals in the freezer. "Whatever I feel like," he said grouchily.

"Never mind, I'll make a grocery list. How do you get the perishables here? In this heat? I guess ice cream is out of the question."

"I take the boat and a cooler," he said. "Anslow is quicker by water."

"You take a boat for groceries?"

"In the summer, yes."

"That's very romantic."

And then she blushed. And well she should. You did not discuss romance with your employer!

"If you make a list, I'll do a run tomorrow." That hardly sounded like a reprimand for discussing romance with him! It sounded like a concession to her feminine presence in his house!

"Oh, good," she said. "I'll be happy to prepare some meals if I have the right ingredients."

There was that whole meal thing again. A strong man would have just said no, that it was not part of her job, and that he was more than capable of looking after himself. But Jefferson had that typical man's weakness for food.

"What kind of meals?" he heard himself ask. He tried to think of the last time he'd had a truly decent meal. It was definitely when he'd been away on business, a great restaurant in Portland, if he recalled. ·

Home cooked had not been part of his vocabulary for over a decade, not since his grandmother had died. How she had loved to cook, old-fashioned meals of turkey or roast beef, mashed potatoes and rich gravy. The meal was always followed with in-season fruit pie—rhubarb, apple, cherry. When he had first moved in with his grandparents, his grandma had still made her own ice cream.

Hailey had been as busy with her career as he himself was. She liked what she called "nouveau cuisine," which she did not cook herself. She had made horrified faces at the feasts he fondly remembered his grandmother providing.

"It is not healthy to eat like that," she had told him.

And yet he could never remember feeling

healthier than when his stomach was full of his grandmother's good food.

Jefferson remembered, suddenly and sharply, he and Hailey arguing about this very kitchen.

"Double ovens?" he'd said, when they met the kitchen designer. *"We'll never use those."*

"The caterers will appreciate it when we entertain."

Why had he argued with her about it? Why had he argued with her about anything? As they had built the house, it had seemed as if the arguments had become unending.

If a man only knew how short time could be, and how unexpectedly everything could change… Jefferson felt the sharpness of regret nip at his heels. Somehow, it felt as if Brook, nosing through his fridge, was the reason for this regret. He usually was able to bury himself in work. It prevented being bothered by pesky emotions and, worse, by guilt.

Brook closed the fridge door and opened the freezer side of the huge French-door-styled appliance. She stood with her hands on her hips for a moment, staring at the neatly stacked boxes of single-serving freezer foods.

"I'll make that list," she said, obviously dismissing everything in the freezer as inedible.

"You do that," he said.

Apparently, she meant to make a list right now, while the lack was fresh in her mind. She found a piece of paper on the counter, and a pen. Her brow furrowed with concentration, and as she wrote, she muttered out loud.

"Chicken. Chocolate chips. Flour. Sugar..."

Chocolate chips. And flour. And sugar. Was she going to make cookies? Jefferson felt some despicable weakness inside himself at the very thought of a homemade cookie.

She had obviously been distracted from her request to see the house. "I'm expecting a call in a few minutes, so if you'll excuse me," he said.

Jefferson eased himself out of the room. His mouth had begun watering at the mention of chicken. Again, his thoughts went to his grandmother and platters of golden fried chicken in the middle of the old plank table.

It was a weakness, but he had no power to

fight it. Besides, so what? She was signing on as his housekeeper, if she wanted to cook a few things, why shouldn't he be the beneficiary? He'd be signing the paychecks, after all. There were no worries that she would be as good a cook as his grandmother had been. No one was that good a cook.

CHAPTER FIVE

As she watched him go, Angie realized that, in her eagerness not to annoy her new employer with anything that could even remotely be construed as chattiness, she had not asked him his name. Now he was in full retreat and she didn't know where his cleaning supplies were kept or where he would like her to stay.

Instead, she watched mutely as he stalked away, down a wide hallway, turned and disappeared from view. A moment later she had heard the slamming of a door.

Considering how unfriendly he was, Angie contemplated what she was feeling. She felt as if she understood his unfriendliness. Her new employer was a man who had lost everything.

For the first time in a long time—far too long, in fact—Angie was aware that it was not all about her. She had seen in his face that he would not brook any sympathy from her, and though her first impulse had been to offer some, she had listened to her instincts. There were other ways to let him know she had heard him and seen him. There were other ways to offer comfort. After the public humiliation of her broken engagement, she personally knew how hollow words could feel.

Her boss had become an orphan when he was six, and now he was a widower. She remembered the shattered-glass look in his eyes when he had revealed that about himself, and his quick rejection of what he had perceived as sympathy even though she had not said a word.

He didn't want sympathy, and she did not blame him. He wanted to be left alone, and she did not blame him for that, either.

But he had let her into his house, and that was a gift to her. She would give him a gift, too. She vowed she would be the best housekeeper the world had ever seen. She vowed for the next two weeks, she would make her employer's life a little bit easier in any way that she could.

Angie contemplated the feeling in her. It was nice that it was not terror. What was it?

She felt *safe*.

Maybe his unfriendliness even made her feel safer. Look where seemingly friendly male interest had landed her last time, after all!

But no matter the reasons, for the first time since she had bolted after finding that stuffed panda on her bed, she felt something in her relax. Really, the tension had been increasing for months, as it became more and more apparent Winston's interest in her was not healthy.

Now, it was as if she had exhaled, after a long, long period of holding her breath. Looking around the neglected house, it felt extraordinary to have a purpose beyond her own survival.

With that exhale came a sensation of pure exhaustion, and she let her eyes wander longingly to the hammock that she could see through the kitchen window. But falling asleep would be no way to make a good first impression or forward her goal of making her boss's life a little better!

She made herself focus on the task at hand. From the stack of leaning mail that had taken over the beautiful harvest-style kitchen table, she presumed his name was Jefferson Stone and that he was a business consultant who owned a company called Stone Systems Analysis. She made a mental note to sort the mail for him. Some was obviously junk, but some of those envelopes just as obviously contained checks and business correspondence.

The kitchen cabinets revealed a rather impoverished selection of food. As she went through the cupboards, her grocery list was becoming quite extensive, especially since the thought of cooking for him now was imbued with her sense of altruism.

After she had finished in the kitchen, she went exploring. Off the kitchen was a laundry room. When she opened the washing machine it had wet clothes in it that had been sitting so long they smelled dank. She found the soap and restarted the cycle. The soap was in a cabinet sadly lacking in the cleaning supplies necessary to keep a house. She retrieved her list and added a few more items.

Moving on, feeling like something of a snoop,

which was ridiculous, she showed herself around the house. Though from the outside it looked as if it was only one level, she took a stairway off the kitchen that led downward to the next level.

It was not really a basement, but a beautiful above-ground lower level, set up for entertaining. It had a billiards table and a bar, but the cover on the table and the dust on the bottles at the bar suggested no one had entertained down here for a very long time. There was a huge TV on one wall. It looked as if Jefferson did watch that, as there were several smudged drink glasses on the coffee table and a bowl that contained the crumbs of potato chips.

There were two guest suites off the entertainment room with fold-back doors out onto private decks that overlooked the lake.

She could choose one to stay in. Both would probably provide ample separation from the master of the house.

But it looked, she thought with a bit of trepidation, as if it would be very easy to break into this lower level. Besides, maybe the photo shoot crew would need a place to stay.

After making a thorough list of what needed to be done downstairs to make it habitable for the photo crew, should they decide to stay there, she scooped up the dirty dishes and went back upstairs. There was no room in the dishwasher for the dishes, and so she started it, stacking a second load above it. It felt beautifully satisfying to be doing these *normal* things.

Then, she crept down the hall the way Jefferson had gone. The first door was firmly closed, and she went on extra silent feet past it. She could hear him talking, and since he did not seem like the type who would talk to himself, she presumed this was the phone call he had scheduled.

And then she went past his office, farther down the hallway. The next door was open a crack to reveal the master bedroom.

She peeked in. There was a huge window that capitalized on the view. Like all the other windows in the house, it needed a thorough cleaning.

A door led to a private deck, where there was a covered hot tub. Another door, closed, must have led to the master bath.

The bed was king size, with a gorgeous solid headboard of gray weathered wood that looked as if it might have been retrieved from an old barn. Still, the room lost any semblance to boutique hotel chic because the beautiful linens on the unmade bed were rumpled. There were clothes on the floor and overflowing the dresser drawers. There was a heap of magazines sliding off the nightstand, and several empty glasses and plates were scattered about available surfaces.

She moved away from Jefferson's open bedroom door, contemplating how relieved she was he had specifically told her to stay out of his room. She bit back a nervous giggle at the thought of what might be in there. *Good grief, she'd been saved from picking up his underwear off the floor.*

"My heart is overflowing with gratitude," she said softly, out loud, and realized it was completely true. She felt as if she had been plucked from a terrible predicament, but more, she had been given a task to do, and she had a sense of being needed, of having a contribution to make.

She kept going.

There were two more guest bedrooms, and a guest bath. The opulence of these rooms was undisturbed. Except for dusting and freshening—and maybe a vase of flowers—they already looked ready for the cover of a magazine.

At the far end of the hall was a narrow doorway. She thought it was a closet, and opened it to see if this was where extra linens were kept.

Instead she found a narrow staircase, and, intrigued, she followed it.

As soon as she saw what was at the top of that narrow staircase, Angie knew this was where she would stay. Her sense of gratitude deepened. The room was a secret sanctuary, octagon shaped, encased in windows. There was even a tiny bathroom through one door. She peeked in at the claw-foot tub, and at yet more windows overlooking the lake. Then she turned back to the room.

It was a delight in whites: white bed, white linens, white walls. The white draperies, on closer inspection, were silk. She was delighted to see the room also had a small craft alcove with a sewing machine and neat cubicles full of fabrics and craft items.

Angie could not help herself. She went over and inspected the sewing machine. It was a very good model. Growing up as she had, in a single-parent household, there hadn't always been money for the fashionable clothes she wanted. But a sewing lesson in a home economics class had changed all that. By the time she was in high school, she could copy any design she saw and was creating her own designs, too. She had made extra money sewing for her mother's friends and for her own classmates.

At home, tucked away safely in a drawer was a sketch for the wedding dress she had designed herself and hoped to wear down the aisle.

That memory brought her back to reality with an unpleasant snap. She became aware it was also unbelievably hot and stuffy in this room, and she went across the bleached hardwood floor and threw open the windows. Within seconds a gorgeous, cool cross breeze was coming off the lake, fluttering in the curtains and cooling and freshening the room.

Though it was not 100 percent in keeping with her mission of making mental lists of what needed to be done in each room, Angie gave in to the temptation to flounce down on the bed. Her flounce created a cloud of dust, but she lay there, anyway, letting the fresh breeze from the windows carry the dust away. She allowed herself to contemplate the delicious sense of being 100 percent safe.

The windows were low, and even lying down she could see the lake. The view from this room was spectacular. She was looking down at the decks below, the one with the hammock on it, and the other with the hot tub.

She blushed at the thought she could spy on her boss while he sat in that tub. He did not seem like the kind who would wear a bathing suit!

"That's exactly the kind of nosey parker he does not want around," she told herself.

She looked away from the hot tub and could see that, beyond the decks, there were rough stairs carved out of the face of the huge stone the whole house sat upon. The steps led to a crescent moon of a beach and a dock with a sleek motorboat bobbing at its mooring. An afternoon wind was kicking up, and there was a chop on the water, the waves white capped.

She knew she could not go to sleep. She could not. But to find safety after experiencing so much tension? To have a sweet sense of mission after floundering in her own distress for so long?

Her eyelids felt as if they were weighted down by stones. She sighed, snuggled into the somewhat dust scented white of the duvet on the bed, and fell fast asleep.

Darkness fell, and Jefferson was edgily aware as he set down the phone after a long afternoon of conferences that he was not alone in his house.

The envelope she had passed him earlier, marked Urgent, caught his attention and he opened it.

Dear Jefferson,
As I mentioned to you in our recent phone conversation, the town of Anslow hopes to

provide a picnic area where the Department of Highways widened the road after your wife's accident. Our intention is to name the area the Hailey Stone Lookout.

Hailey had not been part of our community for very long, but we so want to honor her in this way. Would you please consider attending the fund-raiser as our guest? It would mean a great deal to all of us.

The theme is Black Tie Affair and dress is formal. Dinner with dancing to follow.

Will you let me know?

The letter was signed by Maggie, who as well as running the Emporium, was second in command to the mayor, and the town's most good-hearted busybody.

She, like, Clementine, had been a friend of his grandmother's. She had been one of the ones who circled around him after the death of his parents, clucking over him and loving him through all that pain, sewing him seamlessly into life of a small town. She had cheered at his hockey games and been part of the standing ovation for *Grease*. She had been in the front row, beaming at his graduation. She had held his grandmother's hand when they had buried his grandfather, and again when he had gone away to university. It was Maggie who had held his own hand when he came back for his grandmother's funeral.

When he and Hailey had decided to build on this land that had been his grandparents' it had been Maggie who had welcomed them home as if they belonged here.

Had he already known, even at those initial stages, that Hailey would never belong here?

Jefferson glanced at the date. The fund-raiser was two weeks away, the day before the magazine crew was showing up. He cursed under his breath. It was the second time in one day that honoring Hailey had come up. Just like with the photo shoot, how could he refuse? Plus, he didn't want to let Maggie down. But he had a horrible feeling the whole thing was just a ruse—not to honor Hailey but to parade the whole town's eligible women before him.

The people of Anslow meant so well, but none

of them could believe a life worth living could be had without family. They thought it was "time" for him to get over it and get on with it, as if these things could be done on a schedule. But couldn't they see? For him family was forever connected to loss. And it was loss he could not bear any more of.

"I'll think of a way," he decided. He wished his new housekeeper had never handed him the envelope.

His new housekeeper. He listened. He thought he would hear sounds of her rummaging around, but there was nothing. In fact, he was pretty sure, now that he thought about it, that he had not heard a sound for hours.

He slipped out of his office and into the hallway. Night was falling and his house was in deep shadow. He sniffed the air. He knew there was hardly anything to cook with, so why was he disappointed that she had not made him dinner, and then sharply annoyed at his disappointment.

He had done fine without her for all these years.

He noticed the doorway at the end of the hall

was open, and he went toward it, and then quietly up the dark staircase.

He paused as he came into the room. There was very little light left in it. It had been Hailey's favorite room in the whole house design.

"Like a secret room," she had said.

It had seemed to him it was the kind of room their kids might have adored, back then, when he had still held the hope he would one day create a family of his own.

But Hailey had designed the room not for kids but for crafts.

Crafts? He remembered the astonishment in his voice. Because his wife, the consummate professional, did not do crafts any more than she did double ovens.

The knife ache of pain throbbed along his temples. Because he had had a dream of settling here, and having kids here, and the night that Hailey had run off into the storm, it had been apparent their dreams were entirely different.

He had failed her so colossally.

Then, as his eyes adjusted to the dimness in the room, Jefferson saw Brook on the bed. She was curled up on her side, facing him, and she was fast asleep, her golden sand curls scattered over the white pillow cases.

It occurred to him he should feel annoyed. This was hardly the way for her to make the stellar impression she had promised. And yet seeing her sleeping, the anxiety completely relaxed from her face, Jefferson did not feel annoyed.

He felt as if he had done the right thing, and maybe the only thing. A thing that would have made his grandparents proud of him. This was his grandparents' land. They would have never turned away someone in need. That was the unspoken creed they had lived their lives by, and no one had benefited more than he from their strict adherence to the golden rule.

He stood there for a moment too long, because Brook's eyes opened, sleepy and disoriented at first, and then they widened.

She sat up on the bed. A scream of pure terror erupted from her. She scrambled backward, knees to her chin, pulling the covers along with her and putting her back into the corner.

"Hey," he said. "Hey, Brook, it's okay. It's me."

That apparently was not reassuring, as she screamed again, a scream of fear so primal it made the hair on the back of his neck stand up.

"Jefferson Stone," he said, but then it occurred to him he had not volunteered his name as of yet, so it might not reassure her at all. It also occurred to him, the light in the room was very dim. All she could see was a hulk standing in her doorway.

He stood there for a moment trying to get his eyes to adjust more fully. She scooted out of the corner bed, and he lost sight of her in the darkness. And then something crashed down on his head. By instinct, he reached out, connected with the arm of his attacker and pulled her in close to him.

"Let me go," she screamed, fighting like a wildcat.

Instead of letting her go, Jefferson pulled the panicky woman into his chest and held her hard and tight. She pummeled him with her fists. She reared back and hit his chest with her head. He was afraid she might bite him. But he would not let go.

"Brook, stop it," he said quietly. "Stop it. It's just me. Jefferson."

Finally, his voice seemed to penetrate all that panic. The wriggling strength of her went suddenly still, though he could feel the rabbit-fast beat of her heart against his chest.

"Jefferson?" She tilted her face up at him, and he could see the glitter of gold in her eyes as she stared up at him, frightened and baffled.

"Jefferson Stone, your new boss?"

Silence. And then, recognition pierced the glaze in her eyes, and for the first time he thought she might actually be wide-awake.

"Oh, my God! My new boss. I just hit my new boss with a lamp."

"Yes, you did."

"I'm so sorry. No. I'm beyond sorry. I'm mortified. Devastated. Appall—"

"I get it," he said drily.

She seemed to realize she had made no effort to pull away from him. He realized how delicate she felt pressed into the length of him. He realized what he wanted to realize the least: that his life had become too vacant, lacking almost completely in this most basic of human needs. To be touched.

Jefferson Stone was far too aware that Brook felt good. And smelled good, and that a man could live to see eyes like that searching his face for goodness.

And finding it.

She seemed to realize now that rather than fighting to get out of his arms, she was clinging to him. Embarrassment painted her cheeks a delicate shade of pink. She dropped her arms to her sides and took a wobbly step back from him. After a moment, she lifted her arm and pushed her hand through her rumpled curls.

"I think you should sit down," he said.

No argument. She retreated to the bed. She sat on the edge of it, peering through the darkness.

He reached over and flicked on the overhead light.

Jefferson had never seen terror as naked as what remained in her freshly illuminated face. He held up his hands, like a cowboy who had dropped his weapon, and he backed toward the door. "I'm not going to hurt you."

But now comprehension was dawning in her own features.

"Of course, you're not," she said. "I know who you are now. I thought you were..." She dropped her head into her hands. Her whole body shuddered.

"Are you crying?" he asked. It was the first time since this whole thing had started that he felt panic.

"N-n-no."

Clearly she was lying. Sheesh. She was the world's worst liar.

Jefferson hesitated in the doorway. What he wanted to do was run from the sheer need in her. She was about to hit emotional meltdown.

"I'm practically a hermit," he told her. "I don't know how to help you."

"I—I—I don't need any h-h-help from you."

But she did. She needed, obviously, to be comforted.

He was in no way qualified to do that. His

every inclination was to keep backing up until he was all the way down the stairs.

But what he wanted to do, and what he did, were two separate things.

"Has anyone ever told you that you are the world's worst liar?" he asked.

CHAPTER SIX

"THAT WOULD BE a good thing, wouldn't it?" Brook sniveled. "Being a bad liar?"

In any other circumstances, Jefferson would have agreed with her. But at the moment? He would have liked to believe her. That she did not need any help from him.

Jefferson told himself that rap on the head with her bedside lamp was preventing him from thinking rationally. He was shocked at himself when he did not retreat from Brook's naked need but, instead, dropped his arms to his sides and moved with measured steps into the room, around the shattered lamp and across to the bed.

She looked very vulnerable, still in the blouse and shorts she had arrived in, though now her outfit was quite crumpled. He was ready to stop the second she indicated he should, but she never did. He arrived at the bed, and felt large and oafish, towering over her. She peeked through the fingers that covered her face. She drew in a long, shuddering breath.

She was trembling. It reminded him of aspen leaves in a breeze. Given how frightened she had been, he was sure his very size intimidated.

"I'm sorry," he said softly. "I feel like an ogre in a fairy tale."

She hiccuped, glanced at him through her fingers again and tried for a wobbly smile. "Then I hope it's Wreck."

"I don't have a clue who that is," he admitted.

"*Wreck and Me*? It's a kid's movie about an ogre."

"I'm not up on my kids' movies."

"Wreck turns out to be the good guy, despite appearances." She wasn't sobbing uncontrollably anymore, so he was making progress. Maybe. Did he want her to think he was a good guy? Not really.

Women like her pinned their hopes and dreams on men they perceived to be good guys. Like most, he would eventually let her down.

But not tonight. Tonight he could be a good

guy. He hesitated, looking for a way to not be quite so big against her tininess. And then, seeing nothing else to do, so he was not hovering over her from a great height, he sat down on the edge of the bed. The mattress gave under his weight, and she slid toward him. Their thighs touched. Hers were bare.

A truly good guy would not be so suddenly and painfully aware of her.

She did not try to scoot right through the wall, but regarded him with wide eyes studded with tears.

"So, Brook, who did you think I was?" he asked.

For a moment, she didn't comprehend the name, confirming that she was just about the world's worst liar and that she had lied about who she was. But that lie was somehow connected to this terror and to the tears trickling down her cheeks. Now was not the time to press her for the truth.

"I—I—I thought you were someone else," she managed to stammer.

"That's reassuring." He deliberately kept his

voice flat and calm. "I can be grumpy, yes. But I don't think terrifying enough to deserve a lamp over the head."

"I'm so sorry."

"I've certainly never had a woman react to me like that before."

He saw the faintest glimmer of a smile and was encouraged by it. It was like trying to win the trust of a wary deer in a meadow.

"No, I don't suppose you have," she said.

This was going from bad to worse. She was blushing delicately. She probably would have liked to lie about the fact she thought he was attractive. There was no need for him to preen. He needed to recognize the danger. His housekeeper thought he was attractive. *And* a good guy.

She was obviously going to survive. He ordered himself to get up and leave.

The stupid good guy vetoed him.

"Who?" he asked. "Who the hell is scaring you like this?"

His tone was all wrong, he realized, the fury at whoever it was having crept, entirely unbidden, into his voice. She seemed to shrink in on herself, as if being terrified was an indictment of her, as if somehow her being terrified was her own fault, an unforgivable weakness.

"It was just a bad dream," she said, her voice muffled.

She was lying again. It had not been just a bad dream. But he let it go. He shouldn't have pursued it in the first place. It fell strongly into the *none of his business* category. It was time to extricate himself from this situation.

The good guy was not ready to go. The good guy was struggling to find words to bring her comfort. Of course the colossally self-centered guy had been in charge so long, he could find none. The analyst had long ago banished sensitivity as a weakness that could not be tolerated.

The good guy could not fail to notice she was still trembling, that tears were still slithering out between the fingers that covered her face.

The bad guy in him sighed with resignation and went, somewhat unwillingly, where the good guy told him to go. It was not a place of numbers. Or words. Or equations. Or analysis.

The good guy in Jefferson Stone went to the place where his grandmother had gone when a frightened and heartbroken waif had been delivered to her.

"Are you okay?" he asked.

"Yes."

But she wasn't. Her voice was wobbling as if she was running a jackhammer. She scrubbed furiously at her tears with the palm of one hand.

Some instinct or memory of the little boy he had once been, some primal recognition of what goodness was and what was required of him made Jefferson slide his arms under her and tug her over onto his lap. Her hesitation—a sudden stiffening, a small resistance—did not even last a breath. And then she was snuggled into his chest, her curls tickling his chin, her tears washing through his shirt, her warm weight a puddle against him.

"It's okay," he said. His voice was rusty, unaccustomed to reaching for that gentle note. "It's okay, sweetheart. You're safe."

Sweetheart? Desperation to make her feel better was obviously making him crazy. What was he doing calling her *sweetheart*? But somehow he didn't want to call her Brook, to invest in the obvious lie she had told him about her name.

It added to his sense of craziness that making physical contact with his new housekeeper seemed to be becoming a regular event!

But, at that moment, the good did shine through. Because despite the sweetness of her curves, despite her warmth pooling against him, despite her designated role in his life, despite the lie of her name between them, she felt not like the beautiful woman that she was. She felt only like a frightened child, as he had once been. And he felt only like a person reaching deeply and desperately within himself for the decency to comfort her, as his grandmother had once done.

And so he stroked her hair and told her over and over again, in a crooning voice that he did not recognize as his own, that she was safe. He could feel the tension draining out of her, her muscles relaxing, her breathing becoming more regular, the hard pulsing of her heart slowing.

And she must have felt safe, because she finally said, her voice low and tentative, "You know how you said I'm not a very good liar?"

"Hmm?"

"My name isn't Brook."

He waited.

She sighed as if she were weighing the wisdom of what she was about to do. "It's Angelica. Angie."

He waited, again, to see if she would go on, if she would explain the necessity of the subterfuge to him, but she didn't. In fact, he felt her relax totally, and then her breath came in even little puffs against his chest. Her hair had fallen forward, shielding her face, and when he tucked it back, he saw she was asleep.

He sat there for a long time, afraid to waken her. Finally his arm felt as if it was going numb. He wondered, as he worked his way out from under the slight weight of her, if she had ever truly been awake.

He settled her back in the bed, drew the covers over her and gazed down at her for a moment.

Her face looked relaxed, angelic even, the perfect face for someone named *Angelica*. He bent and kissed her cheek, as if she was a child he had tucked in.

And then he turned swiftly from her, embarrassed by his tenderness. "I hope," he muttered, "neither of us remembers a thing about this by morning."

She had a chance of that. He did not.

He glanced once more at the sleeping woman, then went quietly down the steps and closed the door to the turret room behind him.

Jefferson was aware of steeling himself against whatever he had felt in that room. It was one thing to be a good man. But it was another to care about others. To care about others was to invite unspeakable pain into your life. He would use this incident to shore up rather than lessen his resolve for their relationship to be professional only. He would withdraw himself, as completely as it was possible to do while they were under one roof. Withdrawing was something he was an absolute expert at. After the blow of Hailey's death, he'd withdrawn quite successfully from the world for the past three years.

Though it was now late at night, he was aware

he would not sleep. He went into his office and shut the door. He was in the middle of a contract to revamp the computer systems for the City of Portland. This was what he loved and this is what he could lose himself in: researching, planning and coordinating the selection and installation of the software systems that gigantic enterprises, towns and cities, corporations and businesses counted on for smooth and efficient operation.

He sat down at his computer and sighed with satisfaction at the reassuring world devoid of emotional complexity. This was his world: analysis. Numbers and graphs and statistics appeared on the screen before him.

"Two weeks?" he told himself. "That's nothing."

CHAPTER SEVEN

ANGIE AWOKE IN the morning, bright light embracing her. For a moment, she had no idea where she was. But the ceiling had a display of dancing light on it, the windows reflecting patterns off the nearby water. She remembered the lake. She remembered arriving at the Stone House. And finding this bedroom and surrendering to the exhaustion that had been building in her.

And then, she remembered last night.

She remembered the panic that had clawed at her throat as she woke up to see a man's figure silhouetted in the doorway.

Disoriented, her fears and stresses must have been playing out in her dreams, because Angie had thought, *Winston found me.* She had reached for that lamp and attacked with full force.

But it had not been Winston. She hoped it had all been a bad dream.

But, no, it was all true. There was the lamp, with a large chunk missing from its glass base and the shade completely crumpled, lying on her floor.

It hadn't been Winston. It had been a man she barely knew. It had been her new employer, Jefferson Stone.

Heat raced up her cheeks as she remembered him comforting her even after she had smashed a lamp over his head. When he had climbed onto the bed? That's when she should have protested more convincingly that she did not need him! When he had pulled her onto his lap? That's when she should have put the wall up and resisted with all her might.

But, no, instead, weakling that she was, she had surrendered into it, allowed herself to feel something she had not felt in months, not even with the police.

It was a sensation beyond feeling safe. Angie had felt protected.

Even if Jefferson hadn't said to her, over and

over, that she was safe, she would have felt protected by him. It was not his words that had comforted. Unlike her, he was incapable of lying about who he was. She had felt the truth that was at the core of Jefferson Stone. She had felt the great strength and calm in his physical presence.

She had felt he was that man—that one-in-a-million man—who would lay down his life to protect someone he perceived as weaker than himself, or vulnerable.

Fresh from terrifying dreams—not to mention months of uncertainty—she had not been strong enough to resist what he had offered. It was what she had wanted most since her terrifying ordeal with Winston had begun. To feel safe again in the world.

And after she had felt safe? After she had realized she was in a lovely bedroom at a house on a lake that most people would not be able to find, even with a map? Then she should have told him to go, released him from that primal duty he felt to protect someone not as strong as him.

But, oh, no, she had given herself completely

over to the temptation of being weak. She had relished his presence. The solidness of his chest, that delicious scent that was all his, the tenderness of his hand in her hair. She had lapped up his attention like a greedy child lapping up ice cream, and in the light of morning, that was exceedingly embarrassing.

Had he really kissed her cheek before he left the room? Her hand flew there as if she would be able to feel the evidence of it lingering. She had let down her guard. She had told him her name was not Brook. It was a moment of terrible weakness that had allowed these indiscretions. She vowed there would not be another.

Though maybe that would not be her choice. She had admitted she had lied to him. She had hit him with a lamp! He would be within his rights, in the cold light of day, to ask her to leave. Or at least to demand an explanation.

A half hour later, showered and dressed and ready for her first day of official duties—if she still had a job—she realized her new boss must also have a plan of avoidance. Obviously, she had managed to embarrass him, too.

His office door was shut when she went by it. There was coffee ready in the kitchen, but investigation did not show much else for breakfast. The man did not even have a loaf of bread! There was an empty box on the counter.

She picked it up and read the label. Apparently Jefferson had indulged in a microwavable bean burrito for breakfast. It was quite pathetic, actually.

She remembered her resolve, even before last night's kindness, to make his life better while she was here. Now, standing there holding the burrito box, she committed more fully to that. She would see that he had proper meals and clean clothes, and that every surface of his house shone, reminding him of what a beautiful place he lived in. Maybe reminding him that it was a beautiful world.

That awareness, that it was a beautiful world, had evaporated from her in the past while, too. Maybe, in helping him discover it, she could recover some of her own faith in the world.

A little frightened, Angie realized she was

allowing the most dangerous thing of all into her world.

She was allowing herself to hope.

That hope infused her as she did normal things. She made a grocery list, put dishes in the dishwasher, cleaned crumbs off the counter. It was a testament to how crazy her life had become that doing these small things filled her with such pleasure. She had never really appreciated how wonderful it was to just be normal.

Still, she could not use these simple pleasures as an excuse to delay seeing Jefferson this morning. With her list in hand, she approached his office door. It was true her boss had made it plain he didn't like interruptions, but she couldn't very well ignore the events of last night. And she needed to know if he planned to oust her over her deception about her name.

Standing in the hallway, she was aware her heart was beating too hard. She rehearsed what she would say. If he did keep her on, she needed him to know that his tender concern, while appreciated, was not in any way expected by her. The exact opposite, in fact. She would prefer they stay on less familiar terms. The list was a pretext to get into his office and make her speech.

She knocked.

"Yes?"

She opened the door a crack and peeked in. Jefferson looked exhausted. Here, she had vowed to make his life better, and it was apparent it was already worse!

"You haven't been up all night, have you?" she asked, appalled, her rehearsed speech forgotten.

He glowered at her. "You're my housekeeper, not my mother." His tone was unnecessarily curt.

But all she heard was *you're my housekeeper.* He wasn't firing her!

She was relieved that the tenderness she thought she had experienced last night had been largely imagined. At the same time, she was aware that she was ever so faintly annoyed that he had reached the conclusion, all by himself, that his tender concern would not be necessary in the light of day.

"I just wanted to apologize for last night,"

Angie said, the opening line of her speech. It would be a shame to let the whole thing go to waste. She opened the door a little more, though he clearly had not invited her to.

"No need." He waved a dismissive hand at her. The message was clear—*Leave me alone.*

"I was very tired…" She felt driven to explain, stepping over the threshold into his office. "I'm sure it won't happen again."

"Great," he said. He glanced up from his computer, acknowledged the fact she was actually in his office with a slight frown and looked back at the computer. "I only have so many lamps."

This was very good. He was going to make it about the lamp instead of about her. And him. And embarrassingly tender moments.

"I'll pay for the lamp," she insisted, following his lead. Let's make it about the lamp. Only that was harder than it should have been. Even with that scowl on his face, he was a very attractive man. It was not so easy to dismiss the fact she had been on his lap last night.

"I don't care about it, actually." Apparently, it was easy for him to dismiss it.

"Well, I do. I'll pay for it. I insist."

"Whatever." This was a discharge.

In case she didn't get that, he waved a hand at her, as if she was a bothersome fly. She noticed a lump on his head and stepped in to his office even farther. She didn't stop until she was standing right in front of him.

He looked up from his computer and folded his arms over his chest, clearly annoyed. "You've apologized. We've established you are paying for the lamp. Was there anything else?"

"Are you having any symptoms of concussion?" she asked. "Because you have quite a large lump right—"

She reached for him; he reared back. She snatched her hand away and touched her own forehead above her eyebrow. "Here," she finished weakly.

"I am not having the symptoms of a concussion," he said.

"How's your head?" He had a lump rising above one of his slashing eyebrows.

She thought he would at least express some curiosity about her real identity, but he did not.

"Aren't you going to ask me why I gave you a false name?" she said.

He studied her for a moment. "No."

"Oh." She realized she was disappointed in his lack of interest—not that she wanted to get into the whole tawdry tale of her failure to discern a bad person from a good one. Still, she felt driven to say something else.

"I just want you to know, I'm not a person you can't trust."

He looked at his watch, a hint that she didn't have to say anything else.

For some reason, she babbled on. "I don't have a list of aliases. There is no dead person in an attic somewhere that can be attributed to me. I'm not on the run from the law."

Something like a smile tickled at the edges of his lips. "You think you had to tell me that you're not a murderer or a fugitive?" he asked.

She nodded vigorously.

"It's imminently apparent that you are not."

"That's good," she said, though she wasn't so sure. He had managed to say that as if she had *boring* written all over her, as if she was exactly the kind of woman whose fiancé would leave in search of excitement elsewhere.

"It's also imminently apparent that something, or someone, has thrown a very bad scare into you. If it's a man—" the smile had disappeared completely and something dangerous darkened his eyes "—you need to get rid of him and never look back."

She opened her mouth to say something and then closed it again. Jefferson was already looking back to his computer. It was a man, but it was too complicated to explain, and he clearly did not want an explanation. Despite the advice, he was letting her know that theirs was a temporary arrangement and that she had to handle her life herself. He had absolutely no interest in her personal dramas. He did not want a repeat of last night any more than she did.

Except that looking at him, she did feel a strange longing to see the tender side of him again, to feel his hand in her hair and his lips on her cheek.

'After a moment, he glanced at her, and she realized she was still standing there, trying to reconcile this cold indifference with the man who had comforted her last night.

Yes, that lump on your head, right over your scowling brow, needs some attention. And I would love to finish what I started, to lean over and put my fingers on it, as if somehow I could soothe the pain away. The way you soothed mine away last night.

But he was looking at her like the man least likely to want his pain soothed away. She thought of the little lost boy in that photograph in the living room. And she suspected the lump on Jefferson Stone's head was the least of his pain.

She was glad she had the grocery list and didn't have to make up an excuse for the fact she was standing there staring at him. "You asked me if there was anything else and yes, there is. There's this."

Trying not to feel as if she was scurrying under his impatient eye, she crossed the room and thrust the list in front of him.

He picked it up and studied it. The annoyed scowl creased his brow again. "Good grief, are we supplying a barracks?" he said, lifting his eyes to hers.

"It's really just basics."

He glared again at the list, then lifted those cool gray eyes to hers. "Cumin is a basic?"

His pronunciation of cumin was way off. He made it sound like something quite erotic.

"It's a spice! You don't have any spices," she sputtered. She willed herself not to blush over something so silly as the pronunciation of *cumin*.

"Well, I doubt if they have anything quite so exotic in Anslow. There's no big-box supermarket there. It's a little family general store."

"It's not exotic," she said. Good grief. She sounded defensive over a spice. She was pretty sure she was blushing.

"Well, I'm still not going to go ask for it. People would get the wrong idea entirely." He took a pen off his desk and put a line through cumin.

"They might indeed get the wrong idea if you said it like that." She could not resist commenting. "It's not *coming*." Now her cheeks felt as if they were on fire. "It's pronounced *coo-men*."

"Huh." Unsaid: *I don't give a damn*, though he was watching her face with interest now.

"I use it in homemade guacamole. I make really good burritos. You'll never want a frozen one again." She was hoping to get him to put cumin back on the list and to distract him from her schoolgirl reaction to what was simply a wrong pronunciation.

"That's the problem with improvements," he said. "They make you dissatisfied with the way things were before."

"Well, in terms of frozen burritos for breakfast, that can only be a good thing."

He appeared about to remind her, again, she was not his mother. Instead, he looked back at the list.

"I don't know where any of this stuff is," he said. "Cornstarch. Where do you find that? In the vegetables or in the laundry supplies?"

She pressed her lips together to keep from laughing.

"How essential can something called cornstarch be, anyway? I don't even like my shirts starched. That was my grandfather's generation." He took his pen and struck another item from her list.

"It's for thickening sauces, not for doing laundry," she said, but he did not appear to hear her.

"Dark chocolate ice cream? Not just ordinary chocolate?"

She had been planning on making iced mocha for the heat of the afternoon. In truth, it was all part of her plot to make him *happy*.

It was more than obvious happiness did not come naturally to him. Rather than seeing that as a challenge, she should just admit to herself that she had set an impossible task.

If only bringing someone happiness could be as simple as giving them an iced mocha on a hot afternoon.

CHAPTER EIGHT

"THE ICE CREAM may not be essential," Angie admitted, though she was reluctant to give ground.

"Good." Jefferson crossed it off the list with a little too much enthusiasm, and then muttered, "If I was going to get ice cream, it wouldn't be chocolate, anyway."

"What kind would it be?" she asked, curious despite herself. You could probably tell a lot about a man by the kind of ice cream he liked.

But he only spared her a glance that made her feel as if the question had been highly personal, like asking if he preferred boxers or briefs.

"You know," he said, displeasure deepening his voice even more, "I offered to pick up a few things in town because I have another errand to do there, but a list like this? I'll be wandering in the market for hours. They'll have to send in a Saint Bernard to find me, hopefully with a keg of brandy around his neck. Brandy." He squinted at her list and crossed something off. She was fairly certain it was the cooking sherry.

"I hate going to the market, anyway," he admitted.

"That explains the frozen bean burrito for breakfast."

"Yes, it does," he said unapologetically. "One-stop shopping. I stop at the freezer, fill my basket, and leave. I can be done in forty-three seconds."

"Well, you should at least be familiar with where the ice cream is if you're such a fan of the freezer section," she said. She should leave it at that. Really, she should. But she didn't. "Why do you hate going to the market?"

"These people have known me since I was six years old. They have an annoying tendency to fuss over me," he snapped. "You're not the first person to think my food selections are not that great. All those busybodies peering in my basket."

Not everyone, she guessed. Women. It was a

small town. He was probably its most eligible bachelor. And damned unhappy about it, too. She could just imagine them clucking over him at the supermarket.

She made a note to herself. *No clucking. No fussing.* He was right. She was not his mother.

"There's only one solution," he said.

She held her breath. Either he was going to throw out the list or reconsider her employment.

But as it turned out, there was a third option, which she had not even considered.

"You'll have to come and do the shopping yourself." He held out the list, and she snatched it from him, trying not to show her delight at this unexpected turn of events. "I'll send you off to the market while I run my other errands."

"It won't put you out in the least to have me along," she said. It sounded like a promise.

"Yeah, whatever." He didn't have the grace to appear even slightly grateful she was going to get some decent supplies for him. He glanced at his watch. "I can't go until later this afternoon. Can you be ready around four-thirty?"

She sighed. "That means frozen bean burritos for lunch, I'm afraid."

"You say that as if it's a bad thing," he said drily.

It was when she left his office that she remembered he said he went to Anslow by boat. And she had said she thought that was romantic, even though she shouldn't have done. Anyway, she scolded herself, if that was her idea of romance, it was no wonder that her fiancé had left her for someone who wanted to live on a beach in Thailand!

Well, if she was not Jefferson's mother, she was even less likely a romantic prospect. Luckily for her—and for tired-of-women-fussing-over-him Jefferson—she was completely disillusioned in that department. Harry, and then Winston, had seen to that.

What a relief. Because feeling romantic about her boss in any context, including a boat ride, could lead to dreadful complications, even in two short weeks.

But for some horrible reason, even as she vowed off romance, Angie thought of his lips brushing her cheek the night before. And she blushed even more deeply than she had over the mispronunciation of a word.

She squeezed as much activity as she could into the day. By the time four-thirty rolled around, the dishes and laundry were completely caught up and the kitchen was gleaming. It was hot, though. A thermometer on the outside of the kitchen window told her it was a hundred and two degrees outside when she slipped up to her room and showered the day's grime off.

Angie had hauled her meager suitcase up the stairs to her room. She had not, in her panicked flight from Calgary, packed one thing that might impress Jefferson Stone. It was too hot to impress, anyway. She slipped on a clean white T-shirt and a very simple wraparound skirt she had designed and made herself. Then she ran a brush through hair that was springing up all over the place.

"Ready?" he asked as she came down the stairs.

"Is it always so hot here?" She regarded Jefferson. He didn't look hot at all in a summer sports shirt and light khaki shorts. He looked cool and confident and composed—a man who did not invite fussing at the supermarket.

"This is a pretty average summer day. You could have turned on the air-conditioning."

"I was hoping to freshen up the house by leaving all the windows open. I think I've succeeded only at letting the heat in. How are we going to keep the groceries from wilting?"

We. As if they were a partnership. She contemplated how easily the "we" had slipped from her lips.

He grabbed a large cooler from the storage cabinet by the back door and then led her out the back door and across the deck. She noticed he did not bother locking the door they came out. He paused before taking the stairs down, scanning the nearby mountains.

"What?"

"Just looking at the clouds," he said.

She followed his gaze. The clouds were huge, pure white and fluffy as cotton balls, obliterating the tops of the mountains. "They're beautiful," she said. "Can you see anything in them?"

He cast her a glance, shook his head and snorted.

"Well, I can," she said stubbornly. "It looks like a horse kicking up clouds of snow behind it."

He looked back at the clouds, squinted, then shook it off.

"It's not unusual to get a thunderstorm late in the day when it's hot like this," he said. "Hopefully, it will hold off."

"I don't know. I feel as if I'd love to stand out in the rain right now." The heat was absolutely withering.

He looked as if he was going to say something but, with one more glance at the clouds and at her, changed his mind.

They went down a steep staircase, carved into stone, that led to a crescent of private white-sand beach and to a boat dock. It seemed with every step closer to the water, the air cooled.

"Oh," Angie said, looking at the sleek boat bobbing at its moorings. "It looks like something out of James Bond." Come to think of it, *he* looked like something out of James Bond!

He stepped from the dock to the boat with absolute ease despite the cooler in his hands and the bobbing of the boat.

"Wait," he snapped when she tried to follow. He stored the cooler and came back. He reached out his hand to her, and she took it and leaned forward for the long and rather scary step down. He sensed her hesitation and let go of her hand. Then he put his hands around her waist, lifted her easily into the boat and set her back on her feet.

For a moment they stood there, looking at each other, his hands still cupping her waist. She glimpsed the man he had been last night. Angie had a sense of time stopping, of being highly aware of the way the hot afternoon sunshine felt on her skin and of how it looked in the crisp darkness of his hair. She was aware of the shape of his lips and the moody gray of his eyes, the strength in those hands that practically encircled her waist. She was aware of the birds calling all around them, the annoyed chatter of a squirrel, the gentle lap of water against the hull of the boat.

She was aware of feeling exquisitely alive.

Then Jefferson abruptly released her. He tossed a cover over a seat beside the wheel, and she took it, aware of the scorching heat coming up through the cover. It was the kind of gorgeous white leather she thought was reserved for higher end cars.

He was back out on the dock releasing the boat from its moorings. He tossed the lines in the boat then gave it a shove with his foot before leaping with mountain goat agility over the swiftly widening gap of water between the dock and the boat.

He took the seat beside her, put a key in the ignition and powerful engines thrummed to life.

He motioned to a sliding panel located between their seats, slid it open briefly to show her a staircase leading into the hull of the boat. "Life jackets are in here, if we should need them. And facilities."

There was a bathroom on board? "I've never been on a powerboat," she murmured. "It seems very *Lifestyles of the Rich and Famous*."

He snorted at that. "It's the reality of living

on a lake. I'm afraid the realities of living in a place like this are easy to overlook on a beautiful summer day like this."

She cast him a glance, but his lips were pressed together as if he thought he had said too much.

He snapped the slider shut, then expertly backed the vessel out of its mooring, guided it to the mouth of the bay and opened the throttle.

"But you like it, don't you?"

"Absolutely. But I grew up with it. I understand there are certain hardships and inconveniences associated with living in a remote place."

There was something about the way he said *I* that alerted Angie of something deeper going on.

"Your wife didn't like it," she guessed softly.

"She thought she would, but—" He shrugged. His voice drifted away, and he squinted intently at the water ahead of them.

"But?" she prodded carefully.

He shot her a look. "But she didn't," he said tersely. "Look, there's an eagle."

The fact that he had pointed out the bird to distract her did not make it any less magnificent. She watched, awed, as the bald eagle floated on the wind current.

Then, clear of his bay, Jefferson opened it up. The nose of the boat lifted, and they rocketed across the smooth surface of the water, cutting it cleanly, leaving sprays of white foam in their wake.

"Oh," she called gratefully over the sounds of the engines, "it's as if the air-conditioning has been turned on." She could feel a fine spray of water misting her skin. The wind tangled in her hair. It was glorious on such a hot day. It was so sensual it made her feel almost delirious. Angie laughed out loud.

Jefferson glanced at her, and his gaze held before he looked away. The stern line that had appeared around his mouth at the mention of his wife softened.

"I've never done anything like this before," she called to him over the powerful purr of the engines. "It's fun. Oh, my gosh, this is so much fun."

* * *

Jefferson glanced at her. Angie's face was alight, and she laughed out loud again as he opened up the throttle even more. The boat lifted from the water and then went back down with a bone-jarring whack that sent spray right over the windshield. The wind was wreaking havoc on her curls.

It was so completely different from last night when she had awoken in terror that he gave himself over to it a tiny bit. He was trying his best to hold himself away from her, but her laughter and her genuine enjoyment were an enchantment.

He reminded himself, sternly, what he had said to her this morning.

That's the problem with improvements. They make you dissatisfied with the way things were before.

Jefferson was well aware that Angie could be that kind of problem. She could storm his world and it wasn't just because she was so cute with the wind tangling in her hair, and her T-shirt molded to the front of her, her slender legs shown off to advantage by a red-and-white flowered skirt. It went deeper: her vulnerability and her laughter, her recipes and ideas. She could pry secrets best left untold—like the secret of Hailey's growing discontent with the lake life—from him. She could make him dissatisfied with the life he'd had before she had arrived.

Despite her diminutive size, he was well aware she was a powerful presence. And right now, with the wind catching in her hair and the laughter bubbling out of her? She was beautiful.

In fact, it was dangerous how attractive he found her. He reminded himself of what he had told himself last night. It was an equation, not unlike the equations he put together for companies and corporations. One plus one equals.

And this equation went like this: caring about somebody equaled pain. It left you wide-open to a world of hurt.

And yet, if he contemplated the past few years of his life, where he thought he had evaded more hurt at all costs, he saw a great stretch of emptiness that he was suddenly and acutely aware had caused pain of its own.

He *hated* that. Angie had been in his life one day. It was just a little over twenty-four hours since she had arrived on his doorstep and cajoled her way into his house and his life. And something was shifting. That something was his own perception, which he was aware could be the most powerful thing of all.

Even knowing that, even knowing that he was playing with fire, he could not resist her smile.

"So, you have seriously never been on a powerboat before?" he called over the powerful thrum of the engines.

"Grew up in a place that was landlocked," she said. "It was just my mom and me. We would have never had the resources to go on a boat."

"Where was your dad?"

The carefree look disappeared from her face. "He left when I was ten. It was a shock. Nothing had seemed really wrong between him and my mother. Someone else caught his fancy. He didn't really factor into our lives, much, after that."

"It may be the way of the world," Jefferson said, and he could hear the tightness in his own voice, "but I always feel put out when I hear people have thrown away a family—for something as ridiculous as something or someone else catching their fancy—when mine was taken from me. Do they not understand the value of what they have?"

Angie reached across the space that separated them and laid her hand on his wrist. It was just for a second, a small gesture, but in that moment he felt as if she got it. She got exactly what he was saying.

"My grandparents' generation had many things right," he said. He had inherited strong traditional values from them. He still remembered his shock when Hailey had told him *after* they married that she didn't want children. It was the kind of thing they should have discussed first, but they had been so caught up in the passion they hadn't. And he would have never left her because of it. Never.

"They did have many things right," she agreed.

The mood had become somber, and Jefferson

realized he wanted to make her laugh again. He was ridiculously pleased by the total lack of worry and tension in her as she embraced the mild adventure of a boat racing across a lake.

He gave in to a small temptation to show her how much fun it could be, and began to cut powerful S patterns through the water. The boat was so responsive. It leaned deep into the twists.

Instead of hanging on tight, she threw wide her arms. She held out her hand to catch the spray. She chortled with uninhibited delight.

And a trip that should have taken him ten minutes took double that, as he traveled the long way, cutting big looping S's across the mirror surface of a lake that they had all to themselves.

He finally pulled into the mouth of Anslow Bay.

"It is so beautiful," she whispered.

He followed her gaze to the shoreline. It was beautiful. He felt as if he was looking at it with fresh eyes: the cluster of pastel-colored houses, visible through the thick greenery of trees, climbing up the hills around the bay. A church spire shone brilliant white in the afternoon sun.

But he had seen Anslow from the water a thousand times before. He was aware, again, of the sway Angie was holding on his perception. He dared to glance at her.

She was what was beautiful. He made himself look away, cut back the engines and focus on docking at the public pier that was at the heart of downtown Anslow.

He was almost afraid to look at her, again, and he was annoyed with his fear. Still, he leaped out of the boat and onto the dock to moor his boat. When he looked back at her after fastening the lines, he understood his fear completely. Angie's skirt had ridden up her legs. Her hair was crazy. Her cheeks were bright from wind and sunshine. Freckles were darkening over that little snub of a nose. Her lips were curved up in a delighted smile. And her eyes were shining with a light that a man could live to see.

It was with reluctance that he leaned from the dock and held out his hand to her. As he suspected, when she took it, it was as if an electrical circuit had been completed. His awareness of her was jolting. Her hand was soft in his, and yet strong. He gave a little tug and she flew up onto the dock beside him. He didn't release her. They stood staring at each other.

"There are no words for the way you just made me feel," she whispered.

Because of the boat ride? Or the confidences they had shared? Or the way it had felt, just now, when their hands touched and the circuit was completed?

And then, he supposed because there were no words, she stood on her tiptoes and kissed his cheek, in almost exactly the same way he had kissed hers the night before.

Her lips were as soft as a hummingbird's wings on his skin. He felt that electrical awareness of her tingle right into his belly.

"Thank you," she whispered, and stepped away from him, embarrassed. As well she should be!

You didn't kiss your boss! But, somehow, the words evaporated within him. Instead, he said, "The store is right across the street. Just walk to the end of the pier, go through that gate, turn right and cross the street. Have them put everything on my account."

She wasn't fooled that he hadn't been affected. It bothered him that she wasn't fooled. Then she ducked her head and scurried away.

He touched his cheek. That moment of weakness—of *wanting* to make her happy—had cost him. He knew that. He knew something so small as that kiss could change everything. It could make a man dissatisfied with what he'd had before.

If he let it.

"Hellooo, Jefferson."

He had just left the dock area and was making his way through the summer-crowded streets to the post office. He whirled around.

Maggie. He hoped she had not seen him receiving kisses on the dock.

"I've been hoping to run into you. Are you going to come, Jefferson? To our fund-raising event? A Black Tie Affair?"

Jefferson was annoyed with himself. He'd been so distracted by that damned grocery list, and by Angie, that he hadn't really prepared himself for an encounter with Maggie. For him, going into Anslow was often like running the gauntlet.

He looked at Maggie's face. In its wrinkled lines he saw wisdom and compassion and caring...for him. She was trying so desperately to try to make something good come from something bad. She was trying so desperately to bring him back from the abyss.

A few days ago, he would have made an excuse. He would not have been able to see the naked caring in her face. No. Maybe he would have seen it. But he would not have allowed himself to feel it.

But now, after he had just lectured about people throwing away the things that mattered? But now, after he had made an effort to be better man? After he had comforted the crying, terrified woman instead of walking away? After he had committed to giving her that moment's enjoyment she had not experienced as a child? After he had committed to making her laugh? It was hard to put that particular horse back in the barn.

He reached out and touched Maggie's shoulder. "Of course, I'm coming," he heard himself say.

"Oh, Jefferson, that means so much to me."

Her eyes had tears in them. He was not sure he could handle any more tears this week. He was at his quota. So, he gave Maggie's shoulder one more squeeze and went on his way.

He wanted to believe nothing about him was changed.

But the fact that he was considering *feelings*—those pesky unpredictable things—meant something major had changed already, not needing any kind of permission from him.

CHAPTER NINE

ONCE JEFFERSON HAD turned back to the boat, Angie touched a finger to her lips. She had just kissed her boss.

Oh, it had been a casual thing, an impulse when words had evaded her. She had just wanted to let him know how much she had loved the boat ride, and she wanted to acknowledge she knew he had made an extra effort to make it pleasurable for her. Maybe, she had even wanted him to know, in that brief touch of her lips to his cheek, that she saw, despite how much he did not want her to see it, that he was a good man.

She could tell he felt guilty about his wife not liking the lake, that it was a burden that had become heavier because Hailey had died. Maybe she had hoped that kiss could tell him what she could not: that his guilt was uncalled-for.

It was a lot to expect of a kiss.

And it had rocked her world more than she had expected it to. She had intended a light peck on his cheek, and really, that was all it had been.

And yet she had been so aware of the rough scrape of his whiskers, the sun and water scent of him, the color of his eyes, the easy strength and confidence of him.

"No more kisses on the cheek or otherwise," she ordered herself internally. *Otherwise?* How had that crept in there? But you did not kiss a man like Jefferson Stone on the cheek without wanting more, without contemplating the sweetness of his lips.

Distracted as she was by the pure and unexpected pleasure of the boat trip—and her lips on the roughness of his cheek—Angie made herself focus on Anslow. She had passed through here briefly just yesterday. It was a measure of how fraught with anxiety she had been that she had barely noticed the town.

Now, she saw the sleepy lakeside village was like something you would see on a postcard of a perfect place to be in the summer. The pier jutted out from the main street. That street had a row of single-story false-fronted stores on one side of it, facing the lake. The buildings were authentically old, mostly whitewashed, though some were weathered gray. Oak whiskey casks, cut in half, served as planters, and spilled abundant displays of colorful flowers. All in all, downtown Anslow looked like a set for a Western movie!

Along the wooden boardwalk the Emporium was front and center, but there was also a post office and a museum, an ice-cream parlor and a law office. There was a bookstore and a place to rent canoes and bicycles and, farther along, a barn-like structure that was the community hall.

Apparently, many people shared her view of Anslow's summer perfection, because the main street was currently clogged with tourists. The general store, which billed itself as the Anslow Emporium, was packed with holiday goers. Just a short while ago, the crush of people might have made Angie panic. Today, all that summer happiness cemented her sense of well-being.

Or maybe it was knowing that Jefferson was just a few steps away, going about his errands, somewhere on that boardwalk. Though it might be silly, she felt as if his mere presence in such close proximity was protecting her. It felt to Angie as if he would never let anything happen to her. That made Angie feel as at ease as she had felt in months.

Exploring the shop, which stocked everything from clothing to lawn mower parts to groceries, Angie was taken, again, with how delightful it felt to be normal and to be shopping for normal things. She snooped contentedly through the crammed aisles of the general store with a sense of discovery instead of with the ever-present fear shadowing her.

She came to a rack, a slender portion of which had been dedicated to bathing suits. Angie hesitated. In her rush to leave her apartment, swimming had been the furthest thing from her mind.

But now the water of the lake beckoned on these sultry, hot days. The selection was tiny. The one-piece model was a leopard print with no back that was available in four sizes, small to extra-large. The two-piece selection was not much better: the scanty bikinis were available in two different prints, leopard or red polka dots, in the same four sizes.

She snatched a small red polka-dot one before she changed her mind. He never had to see it, but it would allow her to enjoy the lake. She could pay Jefferson back for it out of her first check.

She almost sighed out loud. Enjoyment had not been part of her vocabulary—or her experience—for quite some time!

After that one impulse buy, Angie focused on her list. While Jefferson had been right that it did not stock anything exotic, it did have all the basics and a nice selection of spices, too. Since getting to the store was not an easy matter, even if it was delightful, she planned several meals in advance. Was it delightful to be normal? Or was it delightful to be planning meals for Jefferson? She ignored the heavy black lines he had drawn through many of the items on the list.

When she got to the checkout counter, there was a stand of movies for rent. The rental period was a surprising two weeks. When Angie saw the movie *Wreck and Me*, she could not resist adding it to the purchases. As instructed, she put them on the Stone House account. The clerk looked at her with interest but asked no questions, for which she was thankful.

Her things were loaded into her cart, which she took out into the bright sunshine. The thunderclouds were building over the mountain and there was an ominous pressure in the air. The heat had become absolutely stifling. There was not a breath of wind.

She began to push the buggy toward the dock, but Jefferson materialized at her side and began to lift bags from it. Between the two of them they got everything down to the boat in just one trip. She stowed it under the deck, absently putting her frozen items in the cooler he had brought while contemplating him. Was he avoiding looking at her? Was it because of that kiss? Should she apologize?

When she came back above deck, he was eyeing the clouds and she could sense a certain urgency about him.

"Ready?" he asked tersely. He didn't wait for her reply. She took her seat, and he ignored her completely, scanning the water and the clouds with intensity of focus. Was she a little disappointed that his terseness might be more related to the building clouds than the building tension between them?

When they came out of the protected bay in front of Anslow, she was taken aback at the change to the water. The wind was quite ferocious out in the open and the water had gone from silky smooth to choppy.

"That was sudden," she said.

"This lake can turn in a hair," he said. Under the gathering wind, the chop deepened. The boat began to feel as if it was climbing in and out of swells.

Angie watched Jefferson's face. He looked grimly determined, but not in the least afraid. And then the rain began to pelt down. Lightning hit the water, seemingly right in front of them, and the thunder was so close that the boat shuddered.

The brightness of the day was swallowed in the darkness of the storm. The heavens opened up and the rain began to pelt down.

"This falls into the be-careful-what-you-wish-for department," he told her.

She remembered saying, when they had set out this afternoon, that she had wanted to stand in the rain. "I'm not at all sorry I wished for it," she said. "It's exhilarating."

He cast her a surprised glance, and she grinned at him. He returned to focusing on what he was doing.

Angie was aware she could allow herself to feel the exhilaration because of him: unruffled by the storm, radiating confidence in his ability to handle it. She experienced, again, the exquisite sense of being protected.

She could feel the electricity in the air; she could feel the pitch and power of the water beneath the boat. After the heat of the day, having the water pour down, soaking her hair and then her clothes, felt lovely and sensual in a way she was not sure she had felt before. She felt no danger at all, only the exhilaration of being on such intimate terms with the storm, of sharing this experience with him.

The boat rolled, and she rolled toward him

and then away. She realized there was no one she would rather be with in these circumstances than him. Despite the powerful twin engines at the back of boat, the boat was bobbing like a cork on the stormy waters.

"Summer storms like this don't usually last long," he called over the noise. "I'm going to pull into one of those coves and drop the anchor. We'll wait it out."

The water calmed as soon as he made it past the mouth of the cove and into its shelter. He dropped the anchor, and they stood side by side watching the fury of the storm out on the main lake. The lightning show was amazing. The echo of the thunder was caught in the steep mountain sides of the forested land around the lake.

Angie was so aware of everything: her clothes plastered to her, and his to him. The rain plastering her hair to her head, and his hair to his head, the water running down her face, and his. The blessed coolness in the air after the heat of the day. The feel of the boat moving beneath

them, as if it were a living thing—a dragon—
that they were riding.

Finally, the thunderstorm moved by them,
though they could still hear it as it pressed down
the lake.

"That," she finally said, "was amazing."

"Yeah," he said, "it was. We still won't be
going anywhere for a while." Despite the storm
passing, the wind remained, and the waves in
the main lake were huge.

Was it wrong to *love* that, to love it that she
could hang on to the intensity they were sharing for just a little bit longer?

"Jefferson?" Yesterday she had not even known
this man. But after she had accepted his comfort, and offered him some of her own? After
she had seen how the man handled a storm on
a lake? Her sense of knowing him deeply was
complete.

"Hmm?"

"We have a problem."

He turned and looked at her. His eyes went
dark as he took in her soaked shirt. She could

see the outline of his chest through his own wet shirt.

"Please, don't tell me the boat is leaking." His tone suggested he knew that was not the problem.

"No."

The problem was that the storm had passed and the electricity still leaped in the air between them.

"What's the problem?"

She looked at the slick wetness of his hair. The problem was she wanted to run her hands through it. The problem was that she wanted to press her wet body against his. She gulped and looked away from him.

The problem, she reminded herself. Her mind was blank for a moment, and then she remembered.

"Ice cream!"

"Huh?" He ran a hand through that wet hair where her own hand wanted so badly to go. It freed droplets that ran down the line of his temple, and then his cheek and his jaw.

"You know you took the ice cream off the list?" she said in a rush. "I bought it anyway."

"Why am I unsurprised?" he said, his voice full of irony.

"And the cooler is not going to prevent it from melting."

"No, it won't."

"That's our problem. We have to eat it now. All of it."

"Sounds like kind of a fun problem to have," he said.

"And since you didn't want dark chocolate, I bought two kinds. The dark chocolate for me, and one for you. I tried to guess what you might like."

"And?"

"Salted caramel."

"I have to know," he said drily, "what would make you look at me and think salted caramel?"

"The contradictions," she blurted out. "Sweet and salty."

"Don't kid yourself. There is nothing sweet about me."

But that, she knew, was a lie. She remembered his tenderness from the night before. She thought of how he had deliberately made the boat ride to Anslow exhilarating. Still, she played along with him. "It was Salted Caramel or Nutty Road."

His lips twitched. And then he laughed. It was no less delightful because it was so reluctant.

"I hope you like Salted Caramel. A lot. Because you have to eat a whole bucket of it."

"We don't exactly *have* to," he pointed out pragmatically.

"I should have got the Nutty Road because only a nut would even consider letting ice cream melt,. Even with the cooler it won't last long in this heat."

Aware that something was easing between them, Angie went below and retrieved the two containers of ice cream. She came back topside and he turned from where he had been digging through a side compartment. In his hand he had one of those Swiss Army combination knife sets. He unfolded it to reveal a spoon.

"We're going to have to share," he said. "Only one spoon."

The danger of the storm had nothing on this: sharing a spoon with him. The new ease between them became laced with something else, something as sensuous and unpredictable as that storm.

Jefferson gestured to a bench seat at the back of the boat, sat down and patted the seat beside him. She took the seat, not quite touching him but close enough to be aware of the heat radiating from under his damp shirt. She set down one bucket of ice cream, put the other on her lap and popped the lid off it. She looked into a vat of chocolate the same color as his hair.

"It's already started to melt," she said.

"That lends a sense of urgency to the whole situation," he said.

She glanced at him and realized he was teasing her. The ease and the electricity braided themselves together even more completely.

He dug the spoon in and then held it, heaping with dripping ice cream, out to her. She moved into the circle of his electricity and closed her lips over the spoon, her eyes locked on his.

Without breaking the hold, he took the empty

spoon and dug it back into the chocolate. Seeing his tongue dart out to free the ice cream from the spoon was way too sexy. But then he was holding the spoon, filled again, out to her. She closed her lips around the spoon, aware that his lips had just touched that same place. Ever so slowly, she tugged the ice cream off.

And then she watched him take that same spoon and dip it back into the ice cream and put his lips exactly where hers had just been. His eyes met hers. He did something exquisite to that spoon with his tongue.

When it was her turn, she did something just as exquisite with her tongue. She heard him give a little gasp of surprise.

And longing.

Sharing that spoon became an exploration of sensuality almost as powerful as a kiss. She was so aware of him: the wet transparency of his shirt, the shape of his lips, the light in his eyes, the solidness of his wrists, the strong columns of his fingers as they held the spoon to her lips.

"So, would you say this ice-cream flavor—dark chocolate—is a reflection of you?" he asked.

She gulped. "In what way?"

"Sweet, but with surprising depth and a hint of mystery."

Was he flirting with her?

"You need to be writing ice-cream labels," she said.

"You write the next one."

He reached over her, and took the second bucket of ice cream. He pried the lid off the salted caramel one and dipped the spoon in. He held it out to her and she took it.

"What do you think?" he said. "What would you put on the label?"

"Subtle, but sensuous with hints of salt." Was she flirting back?

He ducked his head and dipped the spoon back into the ice cream and tasted it slowly, rolling the ice cream on his tongue as if he was at a wine tasting.

"I like it, but—" he dipped the spoon back into the chocolate and then into the salted caramel "—who knows what could happen if you combined two such different flavors?"

Was he talking about ice cream? Or was he

flirting? Whatever he was doing, she liked it. She never wanted it to end.

With her eyes still locked on his, she slid the ice cream off the spoon. The whole experience was so exquisite it was almost painful. She had to shut her eyes against it.

When she opened them, he was sliding a spoonful of the mixed version between the sultry mounds of his lips.

"The ice cream tastes like ambrosia," he said gruffly.

"What does that mean, exactly, ambrosia?"

"Food of the gods."

"That's what we will call this new flavor then, Ambrosia."

And this experience, in her mind, also had a name. Ambrosia. Surely, this was the kind of experience the gods fed on? Not food but the quality of air, and the static from the storm, and the hint of danger between her and him right now.

They ate ice cream until they could not eat another bite. They put the lids on the now melted containers and put them aside. While they had been eating the ice cream, darkness had been sliding over the lake. They sat there, side by side, rocking gently on the waters of the cove, while just beyond them the lake rolled, white tipped and violent.

The waves appeared as big and violent as they had during the storm. The wind outside the cove howled a warning.

She shivered, whether from cold or from eating too much ice cream or from awareness she was not sure. Jefferson went below and came back with a blanket.

Again, he had just one. He tossed it over both their shoulders and pulled it tight around them. The warmth from him and from the blanket crept into her. They were sailors, marooned, and she loved it. Night fell and the stars winked on, one by one, studding the pure inky blackness of the sky.

It was crazy, and beautiful.

Going for groceries by boat was definitely the most romantic thing that Angie had ever done.

She was so amazingly aware of everything: the wind, and his warmth and solidness of his shoulder underneath the blanket and the flavor of ice cream in her mouth. She was so aware of how he was not watching the restless waters of the lake, but her.

"What?" she whispered.

"I'm just trying to figure you out."

"Really?"

"Because it is apparent to me that there's nothing about you that is a shrinking violet. It is apparent to me you are very courageous. So, I want to know what has you so frightened."

"This morning you weren't interested," she reminded him.

"I was interested," he admitted. "I just didn't want you to know I was interested."

"And what has changed?" *Besides everything*, she thought to herself.

"This morning we hadn't eaten ice cream off the same spoon."

She sighed deeply. And surrendered.

CHAPTER TEN

JEFFERSON WAS AWARE of the surrender, not just in her but in himself. Had he actually been flirting with his housekeeper?

No, he told himself sternly, he had not. Being with her had coaxed his more playful side to the surface. Okay, he was more than surprised that he had a playful side, but he blamed the storm for cutting down his defenses, placing them in this predicament where they had to share a spoon.

And sharing that spoon had led to this. The complete collapse of defenses. They were going to share even deeper confidences.

"I'm not a housekeeper," Angie confessed solemnly.

"Yeah, I kind of figured that part out."

"I'm close, though, and qualified. I'm a high school home economics teacher in Calgary."

Jefferson contemplated that. He could feel the truth of it—he thought of her making her lists and organizing his kitchen. He thought of her home breaking up, and her longing. He was not surprised that she had chosen a career where she would teach people how to make a home. And superimposed over this knowledge of her, he thought of the taste of ice cream, mingled with her taste, still sweet in his mouth.

"Or I *was* a teacher," she said pensively. "I don't know when I can go back there." She shuddered.

Jefferson pulled the shared blanket more tightly over their shoulders, pulling her more tightly into him. "What happened?"

"First, I need you to understand *why* it happened."

"Okay."

"I met my fiancé in university."

"Your fiancé?" Jefferson felt the shock of it. And the relief. All the electricity between them didn't matter. She was taken! But his relief was short-lived.

"Not anymore," she said sadly. "We broke off.

That's what made me so vulnerable when…well, I'll get to that. Harry and I had been engaged since the second year of our studies. We graduated at the same time, and both got wonderful jobs. I secured my dream job teaching home economics in high school, he got on with one of the banks. I assumed it was time to take the next step, but every time I tried to set a date for the wedding, Harry would become evasive."

He heard inside himself *oh-oh* but did not say it out loud.

"In fact," she said, her lips pursed with remembered annoyance, "had I been paying more attention, I would have seen the whites of his eyes rolling in pure terror at the mere mention of spending a lifetime with me."

"A lifetime with you doesn't seem as if it should make eyes roll in terror."

Her mouth popped open in surprise. She studied his face, as if she was looking for the lie. She smiled. He realized he was treading very dangerous ground, indeed.

"Finally, he worked up his nerve to tell me the

truth. He had discovered his career in finance was a terrible mistake. He was bored."

"God forbid we should ever be bored," Jefferson said. He tried to keep his tone dry, but in fact, he felt angry.

"And unfulfilled. He had just discovered he didn't want what other people wanted. He did not want a boring life in the suburbs with two-point-five children and a bus trip into work every day. And guess what? He'd already found someone who didn't want the very same things he didn't want and it wasn't me."

"Aw, Angie."

She held up her palm. "Please don't feel sorry for me. I should have picked up on the signs long before I did. And, besides, this is just the story before the story."

"Go on."

"So, in the space of a week, he quit his job and asked me for his ring back."

"He asked for the ring back? That's scummy."

She wrinkled her nose. "Thank you. I thought so, too, especially after he told me he intended to sell it to finance his tickets. Make that two tickets."

Jefferson was forming a very low opinion of a man who would not only ask for the ring back, but tell his ex-betrothed the reason he had to have it. "Loser," he muttered.

"Thank you," she said, as if she had desperately needed someone else to see it. Angie looked adorable all wrapped in the blanket, her hair curling wildly as it started to dry. But when she wrinkled her nose like that? How could anyone have ever pried themselves away from her?

"Thailand," Angie went on, tilting her chin bravely. "That's where he and Loxi—can that possibly be a real name?"

She glared at him as if she expected an answer.

"No, I don't think it can be a real name."

"Not that it stopped her from traveling! How can you even get a passport with a name like that?" Her question was full of indignation.

"I'd like to know," he agreed.

She sighed at his agreement. "Anyway, that's

where he and Loxi had a plan to live on the beach and teach yoga or some such thing."

"I'm sorry."

Her eyes searched his, and her chin quivered. In denial of that emotion, she said quickly, "You don't have to be sorry. I'm just setting up why I was vulnerable. I'm over it now."

He doubted that. He could see she carried the pain of the betrayal as if it were somehow her fault, as if she had accepted her fiancé's abandonment as a judgment of her. That she somehow was not worthy.

"But I wasn't over it then. Right after it happened, I was in a shocked daze. Naturally, in the staff room, my missing engagement ring was noticed eventually. I had to tell people Harry and I were no longer an item. I didn't tell anyone the Loxi or Thailand part. It was too humiliating."

Jefferson thought of her carrying that on her own, trying to keep her head up high, and ached for her.

"Anyway, I went from discussing wedding plans and poring over bridal magazines with two other teachers who were engaged to being the subject of gossip and pity."

She sat very still. She pulled the blanket a little tighter around her and gazed out at the dark waters of the pitching lake beyond the cove.

"There was another teacher there," she said, her voice strained. "Winston."

He saw a flinch crawl along her skin.

"I can't say I'd ever paid the least attention to him besides a casual good-morning. He was quite an unassuming little fellow, given to wearing bow ties."

"Never trust a man who wears a bow tie," he told her.

"Now you tell me."

She gave him a little smack on his chest and continued. "He confided in me that the very same thing had happened to him. I could actually see the tears in his eyes when he said it. He asked me if I wanted to go for a coffee with him.

"It seemed safe enough. My God, he was a fellow teacher. I felt sorry for him. I thought maybe he just needed to talk about it. I actually thought *Oh, look, other people beyond you have problems.* I thought it would be good for me to get out of myself for a bit. So, I agreed. One coffee.

"But I could tell, once we were out of the school environment, that there was something a touch off about him. I'm not sure I could put my finger on it, but it made me uncomfortable, and I gulped down my coffee and left with murmured sympathies about the pathetic state of his personal life.

"The next day in the coffee room, he was entirely inappropriate, sitting too close to me, putting his hand on my knee, touching my hair. It was creepy. I took to avoiding him, even taking breaks in my classroom. But he tracked me down, and I did not want to be in my classroom alone with him."

She stopped, troubled. Her hands were wound together and she stared down at them.

Jefferson could see they were trembling. He covered her hands with his own and felt how shockingly cold they were.

"The more I rejected him," Angie whispered, "the more strongly he pursued me. He bugged me at school. He called me at home. He gave me unwanted gifts. He sent flowers.

"I finally had to talk to my principal about it. Winston was warned to stay away from me. He didn't. It actually got worse after the principal talked to him. Within a few weeks, he'd been fired.

"The phone calls really started to come in then. I changed my number three times. He always managed to get it. Sometimes he'd be raging that it was all my fault. Other times he'd tell me he had forgiven me for ruining his life. Other times he would be crying. Pleading with me to come back to him. Come back to him? We'd had a single cup of coffee.

"I had to involve the police. I had to get a restraining order. He started hanging out across the street from my place, just out of range of the order. I moved to a new apartment with what I thought was better security. Despite all that, he just kept coming at me. I was a wreck. I was as jittery as if I drank a hundred cups of coffee a day. I startled if one of the children came up behind me suddenly. I barely slept, and when I did I had terrible dreams.

"I started to question my sanity. I wondered if I was overreacting. I wondered if I was making things worse than they were. I wondered what I had done to lead him on. I pondered, constantly, what I should be doing differently.

"On the last day of school before summer break, I went home to my new apartment. The door was locked. Nothing seemed amiss or out of place. I went into my bedroom. The first thing I noticed was that my dresser drawers had been opened.

"And the second thing I noticed was that there was a stuffed bear on my bed. A huge stuffed bear, a panda, almost as big as I was. It had a red ribbon around its neck that made it look as though its neck had been slashed."

She shuddered at the memory, and Jefferson tried to contain the pure fury that was coursing through his veins.

"I called the police, and they said they would arrest him…if they could find him. I have never felt such terror or felt so unprotected. I tossed a few things in a bag, and got in my car. I let a few friends know I was going away, and why I was going away, but that I couldn't tell them where.

"Because I didn't even know where I was going. It seemed it didn't matter how far I drove, it wasn't far enough. I was so paranoid I would not use my phone or my bank card. I checked in with the police on pay phones—do you know how hard it is to find a pay phone these days—but there was no sign of him. I began to feel as if he was hot on my heels. I was running out of money and hope. And then I saw your ad."

She was silent for a long time. "And that's why," she finished softly, "in a boat in the middle of a lake, right now, I feel exhilarated. Because finally, I am in a place where he can't get at me."

Jefferson knew he should be relieved that it was not their togetherness filling her with exhilaration. He told himself he wasn't relieved—or disappointed—because the emotion he was feeling drowned out every other one.

He had never felt such a killing fury as he felt

now at the two men who had brought Angie to this point. But he controlled himself. He could see she had had enough of men who could not put her first, whose self-centeredness was so complete they could not control their own impulses in the interest of someone else.

"You can stay," he said gruffly.

"What?"

"You can stay at the Stone House. As long as you need to."

"Oh, Jefferson." Her eyes clouded with tears. "I don't know what to say."

And just like before, when she had not known what to say, she leaned into him. He knew what was coming. He had plenty of chance to back away from it.

"You knew," she whispered. "You knew I wasn't really a housekeeper. You knew I was a damsel in distress."

That was plenty of warning. What was a damsel in distress looking for, after all? She was looking for a knight in shining armor.

And he knew he was not that, even as he could feel the storm quieting all around them. The roar of the wind dropped, and the waters of the lake quieted. He knew it was time to break away from this, but he could not.

He was caught in a moment: the intensity of the storm, the sweetness of the ice cream, the warmth of her trust, his need to protect her, his sudden aching awareness of his own loneliness. All of those things were swirling around in him, making it impossible not to take what she offered.

Her lips.

She offered him her lips.

And he leaned in close and took them.

They tasted as he had known they would. Of chocolate and salted caramel, and of something sweetly feminine and trusting.

Her lips tasted of ambrosia, food of the gods. And he, a mere mortal, could not resist it. And so he tasted her, and he put his hands in her wet curls and drew her more deeply to him and tasted her more completely.

And remembered that another woman had trusted him to protect her and keep her safe and he had failed completely.

It took all the strength he had to draw away from Angie. He staggered to his feet. He knew it was not the motion of the boat making him feel so unstable. He'd offered her the sanctuary of his house for as long as she needed it.

It was up to him to make sure she was not *more* damaged when she left. And that meant he had to be better at controlling his needs than the other men in her life had been. He had to be better at putting what she needed ahead of what he wanted.

Because what he wanted was to explore every road that kiss could take them down, to climb every mountain it promised, to discover every valley, to let it open the possibility of new worlds.

His voice was too harsh.

"I am not your knight in shining armor. I am not anyone's knight in shining armor. Do you get that?"

She nodded, but she looked as if she was going to cry again. He left her sitting there, wrapped in the blanket, and he pulled the anchor and turned on his nighttime running lights. He prepared to go.

The water had calmed, and the stars were like jewels shining in a black velvet sky. The light could not even hope to pierce the darkness of his own self-awareness.

When they got to the dock, he moored the boat. In stilted silence she went below and brought up all the groceries she had bought. She passed him up bag after bag of groceries and, finally, two ruined buckets of ice cream. When he offered her his hand to get out of the boat, she refused it and scrambled up on the dock by herself.

Loaded with groceries, he went up the steep steps to the house. She followed him. In the kitchen he set them down.

"I'll look after them," she said tightly.

"I think you should check in with the police again," he said. "Maybe your stalker has been apprehended."

"I'll do that," she said, that same tight note in her voice. But then her forehead wrinkled. "Do you suppose it's safe to call them from your line?"

Jefferson could not even imagine being this

afraid. For a moment, his every defense was undermined. He just wanted to take her into his arms and soothe her, kiss away that furrow from her brow.

Instead, he managed to strip all the emotion from his voice. "I have no doubt your stalker is insanely clever, but I somehow doubt he has managed to tap a police line."

She nodded. "Yes, of course you are right. I will call them in the morning. If they've apprehended him I can go right away."

He barely knew her! How could he possibly be aching at the emptiness she would leave behind?

"And, regardless, I won't stay beyond our original agreement, despite your kind offer," she said, reading between the lines. He would shelter her as long as he *had* to. "I will get the house ready for the magazine, and then I'll go. I can't let this thing go on indefinitely."

He wanted, again, to sweep her up in his arms, to not let her feel she had to deal with *this thing* by herself. But what thing couldn't she let go on indefinitely? Her thing with the stalker or her thing with him? He wanted to finish what they had started.

But wouldn't that be all about what was good for him? Filling some gaping hole inside him? It wouldn't be about what was good for her. He was thankful she was putting a time limit on her stay, even though he had foolishly told her she could stay forever.

Forever.

He could imagine forever with a woman like her. He could imagine starlit boat rides and facing storms. He could, all too easily, imagine campfires on the beach. And decorating a nursery.

But again, that was about some need in him that he had managed to outrun for a long time. He did not deserve that life. He had had his chance at forever. He had even vowed it. And he had not lived up to those vows. He had blown it completely.

But for two weeks? What was that in a lifetime? For two weeks, he could be the better man. Even if that meant staying the hell out of her way.

CHAPTER ELEVEN

ANGIE WATCHED JEFFERSON stalk away and heard the far-off slam of his office door. She sank into a kitchen chair, stunned by all that had transpired since she had climbed on that boat with him in the pre-storm heat of the afternoon.

She touched her lips, and it was as if she could still feel the electricity of his kiss there. The intensity that had leaped up between them had been just like that storm—just as powerful and just as unpredictable.

She could not believe she was capable of being swept away so completely in such a short time. She had known this man just a little over a full day. It wasn't rational to feel so strongly about him.

But that was what storms did. They came unexpectedly. They swept in, sucked everything into their vortex and swept back out, leaving a trail of destruction.

Or maybe not always destruction. The storm that had just passed over Kootenay Lake had probably also left life-giving water on the surrounding forests and land.

Still, Jefferson had been right to pull away. Hadn't he? Despite the sense of intimacy nurtured by being stranded together in the boat, by facing into the teeth of that storm, by sharing buckets of ice cream and the same spoon, they barely knew one another.

On the other hand? So what? What did knowing each other have to do with anything? Angie had been rational her whole life. She had been mapping out carefully the life she wanted since the divorce of her parents when she was a child.

She wanted the sense of safety and security that being part of a family had given her, before the split of her parents. She had determined that solid, unexciting Harry was exactly the kind of man to pin those kinds of hopes and dreams on.

She had *known* him. She had known he woke up at precisely seven-ten every morning. She had known he would always order grilled cheese at the university cafeteria. She had known he preferred the news over *The Big Bang Theory.* Angie had thought that what she had shared with Harry was intimacy and that it would lead her directly to the safety she craved. She had thought their entire lives were predictable enough to make her comfortable.

But in that boat, sharing a spoonful of ice cream with a near stranger, she had felt as if she was digging into the tip of the iceberg that was intimacy. She had felt exhilarated by the potential for danger, not afraid of it. In fact, the exhilaration was in part because, for the first time in far too long, she had not been afraid. She had been the opposite of afraid.

She had been fearless.

And she knew that feeling of being fearless was not going to go willingly back into its box.

She glanced at a clock. It was really too late to do anything and yet she felt too energized by her encounter with Jefferson to go to sleep. She unpacked the groceries and put them away, smiled at the video of *Wreck and Me.* If she left it out for him to find, would he watch it?

Still filled with a restless kind of energy once the groceries were stowed, Angie decided to make some blueberry muffins.

"If he gets nothing else from my stay here, he will be able to see there is life beyond bean burritos," she muttered to herself.

Three days later, Jefferson felt like a prisoner in his own house, marking x's on his wall. He was well aware that in the course of human history, three days was a very short time.

But in the context of having Angie aka Brook Nelson under the same roof as him, it was a torturous eternity. In his efforts to avoid her, she had driven him underground. He'd always enjoyed working at night; now it felt compulsory.

But despite seeing her only occasionally—her crazy hair hidden under a babushka obviously of her own invention, her legs looking long and coltish in shorts and skirts, T-shirts clinging to her, the sweat beading on her neck, the cobwebs sticking to the rubber gloves she always wore—

there was no pretending she was not here. Even though she seemed to be avoiding him just as scrupulously as he was avoiding her, the house smelled different since she had arrived.

If it was just the smell of cleaning supplies and fresh air, it would not have been so disturbing. But no… Her scent—faintly spicy, clean, feminine—clung like a faint vapor in every room she had been in. Which, as far as he could tell, was all of them, except this room and his bedroom.

Also disturbing was the noise. If it was just the noise of the vacuum cleaner and the dishwasher and the washing machine and dryer, it probably would not have been so disturbing. But, though she was probably not aware of it, the more involved she got in some task, the louder she hummed.

Christmas tunes, of all things. "Jingle Bells" and "Here Comes Santa Claus" and "Silent Night." On more than one occasion she had burst into bloody song and it had stuck in his head—*Here comes Santa Claus, here comes Santa Claus, right down Santa Claus lane*—long after she had moved out of hearing.

The problem was she sounded so happy that he could not bring himself to tell her to stop. Even though he was avoiding her with all his might, on those occasions when he could not avoid bumping into her, Jefferson could see the tension she had arrived with had eased from her.

She was still easily startled—he'd come up behind her one day while she was vacuuming, and his eardrums were still ringing from the scream—but was losing that terrified, hunted look he'd first glimpsed on her first day when the pinecone had dropped on her car.

It was not just that the house was undergoing a transformation, which it surely was. Dust was disappearing. Cobwebs were being banished. Floors were emerging from under a layer of grime. Windows were, one by one, beginning to shine.

The biggest transformation was in his kitchen. The day's mail was neatly sorted. Every surface was gleaming. Every dish he left there in the dark of night was swept away. The fridge had real cream in it for his coffee, and milk for the selection of cereals that had appeared. There were single-serving containers of yogurt, and lettuce and tomatoes. There was a selection of drinks. There was fresh fruit in a bowl on the counter.

Best of all—or perhaps worst of all, depending how you looked at it—were the meals that she left for him. Though the heat was climbing into the nineties and was over one hundred again, once, every day she had the oven on for something.

The rich smells tantalized him even before he took his nocturnal journey down to the kitchen to see what she had done. Muffins. Fresh bread. Cookies. Last night, she had left him a roast chicken dinner.

Tonight she had left a steak, and a tinfoil-wrapped potato with careful instructions how to grill it.

He set down her note, aware he felt like a wild animal being lured in by the promise of food. His anticipation for what she would make for him grew every day.

If she wanted to discuss things with him she left him a note. He was uncomfortably aware that he was looking forward to the notes as much as the food. He looked around for today's and found it next to the stack of other ones.

He went through the old ones, aware he was smiling. Hers…

Have you got a ladder I could use outside?

His…

DO NOT UNDER ANY CIRCUMSTANCES GET ON A LADDER.

Would tomorrow be a good day to put the furniture out on the deck for an airing?

DO NOT UNDER ANY CIRCUMSTANCES TRY TO MOVE THAT FURNITURE BY YOURSELF.

I have a system figured out.

NO.

Tonight, he read her response to that, aware he was looking forward to it.

I'm going to put the couches on dishcloths, like coasters, and slide them across the floor. Must you write in all caps like that? It's disconcerting.

NO, YOU AREN'T, he scrawled with great enjoyment. AND YES, I MUST WRITE IN ALL CAPS. I FAILED PENMANSHIP IN SCHOOL.

He hesitated. Too much information? Stop analyzing everything. Admitting he'd failed penmanship in school was not the same as admitting he'd had a terrible row with his wife, and she had gone out into a storm…

He shook that thought off. A gentleman would offer to help Angie move the furniture.

But no, the two weeks minus the time elapsed would be so much easier to get through if he stayed on his path of avoidance. It was good, anyway. He was way ahead of schedule on the Portland project.

He went out to the deck and lit the barbecue

as per her instructions. He stood there for a moment, taking in the dark surface of the lake, the lights across the way, the night sounds. It occurred to him it had been a long time since he had felt something like this: just simple enjoyment.

It occurred to him, even though she wasn't beside him, that she was here. In his house. And somehow, it was changing everything. He wished she was down here with him.

He forced himself to suck it up. To repeat his mantra. *Two weeks. Two weeks. Two weeks.*

Angelica surveyed the kitchen with satisfaction. The early-morning light poured through the windows. Jefferson had eaten his steak dinner and gobbled up the cookies she had made yesterday.

She looked for his note, read it and smiled. He'd failed penmanship? Really, it was hard to imagine him failing anything. She put that note with the others, aware she was collecting them.

She went over to the grinder, and put in coffee beans. In a few minutes fresh coffee was dripping into the pot. She savored the smell of it and the light and the birdsong—and Jefferson's note. She felt so supremely rested. She felt alive and happy.

The phone rang, as she poured herself that first cup of coffee, and she felt herself tensing. Jefferson's house phone rarely rang. For too long, the phone ringing in her life had meant the sound of breathing on the other end. Or a hang-up. Or a sobbing explanation. Or a begging plea.

She reminded herself she was fearless now and, coffee in one hand, she picked up the phone without checking the call display.

"Stone House," she said cheerfully.

A moment later the cup, filled with coffee fell from her hand and shattered on the floor. She stared at the mess, put the phone receiver back in its cradle. She wondered, dazedly, if proclaiming herself fearless had been like a challenge to the gods.

Jefferson appeared at the kitchen door. "I heard a crash." He took in the smashed coffee cup. "Thank God," he said. "I thought you'd finally managed to fall off a ladder."

She shook her head mutely.

He crossed the room in a single stride and gazed down at her.

"What is it?"

"The police just called," she managed to croak. "The Calgary police. I took your advice and called them after..."

That magical night shimmered, momentarily, between them, like a mirage.

And that's what it was, she told herself. A mirage. Real life was different. "Angie?" He took her shoulders and gave her a gentle shake. She looked up into his eyes, and tried to feel the sense of safety she had felt that night, and really ever since. But maybe that had been part of the mirage, feeling safe in an unsafe world.

"Tell me what's happened," he ordered her.

"You know that girl Winston told me he had been dating? The one who supposedly dumped him at the same time Harry dumped me?"

He cocked his head at her, frowning, still holding her shoulders, thank God, anchoring her to his kitchen and him and not allowing her to fly toward her fear.

"She's missing. The police suspect foul play. And they suspect Winston is connected to it, and no, they have not located him yet."

He said a word under his breath that should have appalled her. Instead, for a reason she couldn't decipher immediately, it made her feel reassured, but still she trembled. She could feel panic quaking within her, just below the surface.

"I feel I need to do something," she said. "But I don't know what it is. Scream? Cry? Lock myself in the bathroom? Run away?"

"You aren't doing any of that." He pulled her in close to him and held her tight.

In the circle of Jefferson's arms, she could feel the trembling begin to subside. "I'm not?" she whispered.

"You aren't going to scream, or cry. You aren't going to lock yourself in the bathroom, and you most certainly are not going to run away."

She sighed against him. She wasn't so sure

she wasn't going to cry. "I—I—I guess you're stuck with me for a little while longer, then."

He put her away from him, at arm's length.

"Well," he said, all business, "let's make the most of it, shall we? Did you want to move furniture today?"

She stared at him, stunned by his sudden change in demeanor. "What?"

"Look, I'm not letting you move it by yourself. The last thing I need is a Workers' Compensation claim. And I happen to have a clear day as far as my schedule goes."

Her mouth worked soundlessly. Suddenly, she knew exactly what he was doing. Somehow he knew if he left her alone or even let her make her own decisions, they would all be bad ones. He could probably tell she was a hair away from dissolving into hysterics. Somehow he knew he had to get her focused on something else.

"You should have something to eat. I can recommend the chocolate chip cookies," he said it as if it was an ordinary day.

"Chocolate chip cookies are not breakfast!"

A tiny smile played along his lips, satisfied.

He had managed to distract her, and he was pleased about it.

"I had them. I seem to be okay," he said. He held one out to her, wafted it underneath her nose.

She grabbed it from him and took a bite. Surprisingly, it felt as if it might not be such a bad breakfast, after all. She gobbled down three of them. Surprisingly, it felt as if the knots of anxiety in her stomach were eased. By the cookies, or by him, she couldn't quite be certain.

While she ate cookies, he went and surveyed the living room.

"I have a plan," Jefferson announced. "I have a furniture dolly out in the shed. I think it might work better than the dishrag system you outlined."

She was ashamed of it, but she could not even let him out of her sight when he went to get the dolly.

"You might as well come with me," he said, as if it was his idea, as if she was not already stuck to his heels like glue. "There are other things we might need from the shed."

She followed him outside into the morning. She stopped for a minute, gulping in the freshness, the call of the birds, the chatter of an indignant chipmunk.

At the shed door, he stopped and looked back at her.

"Something else?" he said quietly. "He's not coming for you here. And if he did, he'd have to get past me. And you know what?"

She shook her head.

"He's no match for me."

And she knew, looking up at him, that that was absolutely true. She knew why she had been reassured instead of appalled by that dreadful word he had said.

Because in that single syllable had been this message.

Jefferson Stone would lay down his life for her. And though Angie had lost the lovely sensation of fearless that she had felt over the past few days, something in her relaxed as she watched him fling open the shed door.

"There it is."

She saw the red handles of a dolly poking out

from behind a weed whacker, a sack of lawn seed and several boxes. It seemed to her that her idea of sliding the furniture out of the living room was better than his, but she said nothing.

She reached to take the first dusty box from him. Their hands touched. His closed around hers and squeezed. She realized Jefferson was offering her his strength until her own returned.

CHAPTER TWELVE

ANGIE WAS FEELING STRONGER, already, as she set down the first box, and Jefferson passed her another. Finally, he unearthed the dolly and managed to wrestle it out of the shed.

He brushed himself off while she looked at the dolly. "It's covered in spiderwebs. We just need to—"

She caught Jefferson taking a giant step back out of the corner of her eye.

"What?"

"I don't like spiders," he said.

"You're kidding, right?"

He made a face. She was aware he was not kidding, not entirely.

"For someone who does not want to be mistaken as a knight in shining armor, it was a very brave thing to go inside that shed if you're afraid of spiders."

"I don't recall using the word *afraid*."

"Maybe we're all afraid of something," she said gently.

He rejected her gentleness. "I'm not afraid of them. I just don't like them."

"Look! There's one crawling up the handle. It's huge."

"Don't touch that!"

She ignored him and let the spider crawl onto her hand.

"Put that down."

"He's cute. Look." She held out her hand.

Jefferson stepped back. She stepped forward. He scowled. She giggled. She took another step forward. He retreated, then turned on his heel and darted through the trees.

She shrieked with laughter and went in hot pursuit of him. He plunged through the trees and leaped over fallen logs, shouting his protests.

She followed on his heels, shouting with laughter.

Finally, when they were both gasping for breath from running and laughing and leaping logs and dodging trees, Jefferson put the huge trunk of a live tree between them. He looked out from behind it. She lunged one way. He went the other.

Then his hand snaked out from behind the tree and grabbed her wrist.

"You made me drop him," she protested. In actual fact, she was pretty sure she had dropped the spider a long time ago.

"Thank God," he said. He threw himself down on the forest floor and lay on his back, his hands folded over his chest as if he was monitoring the hard beating of his heart. "It's already hot," he said.

It felt like the most natural thing in the world to lie down on the forest floor beside him. It smelled of new things and ancient things, blended together perfectly. She looked up through the tangle of branches at a bright blue sky. And then she turned her head to look at him, drinking in his strong and now so familiar profile.

New things. The way she felt about him.

Ancient things. The way men and women had come together for all time and against all odds.

"Are you really afraid of spiders?" She suspected he wasn't. He wouldn't be lying here in all this forest duff if he was afraid of creepy-crawly things, would he? "Or were you just distracting me from my own fear?"

"Maybe you were right. Everybody's afraid of something."

"What are you afraid of? Really?"

He was silent for a long time. "Isn't it obvious?" he asked quietly.

She thought of that. She thought of him being an orphan and first losing his grandparents and then his wife. She thought of his extreme isolation. Of the fact that he didn't even want a housekeeper who was chatty.

He was afraid to let anyone in. He was afraid to lose anything else.

"Yes," she said, "it's obvious."

"It's too hot to move furniture today," Jefferson announced, obviously not prepared to probe his fears any further, obviously fearing he had already said way too much. And so there it was. Full retreat.

Except it wasn't. She recognized a miracle when it was presented.

"You want to go out on the boat?" he asked softly.

Angie thought of the boat and how safe she had felt there through the storm, and how much it must have taken for him to offer her this. She thought of the boat as the place where pure magic had unfolded between them.

"Yes," she said. "I want to go out on the boat. And suddenly, I'm starving. I knew cookies were not a good breakfast! Should I pack a lunch?"

"Sure. And don't forget your bathing suit."

"How do you know I have one?"

"It was on the bill."

She thought of that bathing suit. She was pretty sure she did not have the guts to wear it in front of him. On the other hand, he was testing his courage. Maybe all of it, all of life, was a call to courage.

He got up and held out his hand to her. She took it and he never let it go as they walked to the house together.

* * *

"What is that?" Jefferson asked, when Angie met him at the boat a half hour later.

"What?"

"What you are wearing."

"It's a bathing suit cover."

"It looks like a cross between a monk's frock and Mexican serape. Where did you unearth it?"

"I made it," she said, as if she was quite pleased with herself. "I mean I didn't sew it. I didn't have time. I just found some fabric and cut it. I've always been good at making things."

"Hmm, *good* might be a bit of a stretch," he said, and realized he felt comfortable teasing her. It was a terrible thing, but he felt glad about that phone call this morning. It had broken the impasse he had created between them.

He wanted to give her—a woman who had suffered just a little too much—carefree days of summer. He wanted to do that, even if it cost him.

He took the boat out onto the lake, and they did a tour of some of its hundreds of miles of coves and inlets and arms. And then he brought them back to a place that was not that far—and yet a world away—from where his house was located.

"Let's go ashore here for lunch," Jefferson suggested.

"What is this place?" Angie asked, handing him the picnic basket and then taking his hand and letting him help her out of the boat.

"Watch the pier. It's a bit rotten. This is where my grandparents' house used to be. You can still see the foundation."

She wandered over and looked at the crumbling stone foundation. "What happened to the house?"

He went and stood beside her, nudged a stone with his foot. "It burned down a few years ago. It had been abandoned for some time."

"What a beautiful spot." She reached for the basket and pulled a blanket from it. She set it out and they both settled on it. "I'm surprised you didn't build your new house here."

"It wasn't practical. This spot is nearly inaccessible by land. My great-grandfather ran a trading post here for lake traffic. When I came here, my grandparents were still almost exclusively using a boat for transport."

"How did you go to school?"

"Until high school, by correspondence. Then, my grandparents bought a place for us in Anslow. They said it was because they were getting older, but I know it was so I could have a normal high school experience, make some friends." He grinned at the memory. "Meet a girl. My grandfather was always concerned about me meeting a girl."

It occurred to him his grandfather would be very pleased, indeed, to see this girl eating a picnic lunch by the old homestead.

"What kind of normal did you have here?" she asked.

He thought he should probably stop talking, but on the other hand, it was good to distract her and to see her growing more relaxed by the minute.

"The best kind," he said. "I grew up using a boat, and chopping wood and hunting and fishing. I knew every inch of these woods. It helped me. It healed me."

He was shocked to hear himself say that. He was not sure he had ever said it before. If he had been able to say it to Hailey, would she have understood?

"I could never sell it," Jefferson heard himself say.

"Sell it?" Angie looked at him, astonished. "I think it would be criminal to sell it."

As they ate lunch, she seemed to know all the right questions. And so he found himself talking of things he had not spoken of for years. He told her of the basset hound named Sam who had followed him through the days of his boyhood, and of a baby squirrel he had bottle-fed. He told her of the winter the snow had piled up past the roof, and of being on the lake in twenty-foot swells. He told her of bear encounters and afternoons in the hills picking gallons of huckleberries that his grandmother turned into pies and preserves.

"People see this place as magical in the summer, but my favorite time of year here was Christmas," Jefferson said.

"Really? Why?"

"My grandmother used to have a Christmas gathering every year, right on Christmas Day. She sent out a blanket invitation. Everyone was invited, and everyone came. My grandfather and I were put to work a month in advance. We had to find the perfect Christmas tree, and make sure there was enough wood to have a bonfire down by the lake. The main body of this lake never freezes, but sometimes the arms do, and I can remember my grandfather going out there with a saw, every day in December, to check the depth of the ice. We were allowed to skate if the ice was over four inches thick. The day he pronounced it safe was better than Christmas for me. I can remember skating on it when the ice was so clear it was like skating on a sheet of glass over the water.

"It could be hard to get here in the winter, but they came for the Stone Christmas, anyway. There were no gifts allowed at her gathering— my grandmother said the gift was each other. And so people came from miles around, and the women got around her gift rule by bringing pies and homemade bread and buns and jars of preserves.

"Families prepared skits, and we sang songs, and we ate food until we could barely move. We kept a bonfire going, and there was sledding and snow fights and snowman building competitions. Lots of times people came prepared to stay, and there were sleeping bags on the floors, and the gathering lasted for days."

It seemed, as he spoke, he was being restored to some part of himself that he had forgotten.

"It sounds wonderful," she said wistfully. "What happened to it?"

"We had a smaller version of it once we moved into town. My grandparents got older, families grew up and people moved. It just kind of faded away."

They sat there in silence for a long time.

"Are you up for a bit of a hike?" he asked. "There's something I'd like to show you."

He contemplated that invitation, even as he took her hand. He'd never taken anyone to his secret place before. Hailey would not have wanted to go. She would have complained incessantly about bugs and branches snagging her clothes. She would have worried about bears and cougars and wolves.

He guided Angie to a trail that was sadly overgrown, though the animals still used it, so it was passable. Even though her footwear was entirely inappropriate—a flimsy pair of flip-flops, she was uncomplaining as they wound their way steadily upward through the forest growth and the steadily increasing afternoon heat.

The trail ended an hour later at a waterfall. It cascaded out of a rock outcropping fifty feet above them and ended in a gorgeous green pool.

He watched, not the waterfall, which he had seen a thousand times, but her.

Her face was a study in wonder.

"This," she declared softly, "is the most beautiful place in the world."

They were both hot and sticky after the hike, so he stripped off his shirt.

"Ready to swim?" he asked her.

She hesitated and then tugged the hem of that serape/frock invention over her head.

He was aware his mouth fell open. He snapped

it shut. He ordered himself to look away. He didn't.

"Sorry," she said. "It's all they had at the Emporium."

Sorry? She was a goddess. She was a vision. He had to turn from her and dive into the water to break away from the spell she was casting on him in that tiny polka-dot bikini.

He surfaced. She was standing at the edge of the pool. Her arms were wrapped around herself. She was a self-conscious goddess.

"Come in," he called.

She stuck her toe in and emitted a very ungoddess-like shriek. He swam over to her, took the flat of his hand and splashed her.

"Hey! I'm getting in my way. It's very cold."

"It's mountain fed. Of course it's cold. Get in."

"Quit being bossy."

"I'll be bossy if I want. I'm the boss."

She giggled at that. "I'll have to look at my contract," she said, putting a finger to her chin and tapping. "I'm not sure if you're the boss here, or just in the house."

He exploded from the water, wrapped his

arms around her, and fell backward into the pond, taking her with him.

She broke from his embrace and the water, sputtering wildly and shaking water droplets from her curls. She glared at him. She stomped toward him. He moved away. She moved after him.

"Come back here," she demanded.

"That seems as if it would be foolish," he said, moving a bit farther from her.

What he knew, and she didn't was that the floor of the pond dropped away suddenly. He took one more step and was treading water.

She took one more step and was in over her head. When she came up for air, paddling to keep her head above water, the laughter rumbled up from someplace deep inside of him. It felt so pure and so good.

"I'm going to get you," she said.

"If you can catch me. You couldn't this morning. I don't see what has changed."

"You are infuriating."

"Yes, I know." He splashed her.

"Oh!" She plunged after him.

Now that the bathing suit—or lack thereof—was hidden by the cool, pure water, the same playfulness that had been between them with the spider erupted again.

He wanted to keep her from thinking of that phone call. And he wanted to make her laugh again.

Soon they were chasing each other around, splashing and shrieking. Their laughter rang off the walls of the mountains surrounding them and echoed in the rocky cavern behind the waterfall.

Finally, he allowed himself to be caught, and good-naturedly suffered a decent splashing. He guided her under the water of the falls. They could stand up here, and he helped her find her feet. He put his arms around her naked midriff to steady her against the pummeling of the water. She lifted her face to it. And he lifted his.

He stood there, in awe of it, of being baptized by mother earth, cleansed, purified, as if he was being prepared for a new beginning.

Finally, cooled, drenched, pleasantly exhausted,

they dragged themselves out onto a huge sun-warmed rock beside the pond. They lay there side by side, until their breathing had returned to normal.

She reached out and laid her hand on his naked back as if it was the most natural thing in the world.

"I never want to leave here," she said.

And he heard himself saying, "I don't, either."

He closed his eyes. He let the energy ooze from her hand like heated oil, thick and healing, onto his back. And then through the skin of his back and inside of him, bringing light to a place that had been in darkness.

And days later, he knew the place had not been about the waterfall, because they had left the waterfall and yet that feeling of a warm energy, of something deeply comfortable and playful, remained between them.

Jefferson told himself he was allowing this to happen only because he was being a better man. He was distracting Angie from the pure terror of discovering her predecessor in Winston's affections had gone missing.

But somehow it wasn't a job he was doing. There was a kind of joyous discovery of the world they were sharing. His world was boats and water and woods and waterfalls. They took the boat out; they swam, they picnicked, and one memorable afternoon he taught her how to catch a fish. In the perfect marriage of their worlds, she taught him how to cook it.

After the success of that, she invited him into her world even further. He could see what an amazing teacher she must be as she taught him how to make cookies and the correct way to do his laundry and how to sew on a button.

"When I have young guys in my class?" she said. "I consider it my obligation to their future wives to make sure they have a few rudimentary skills."

Who would have guessed gaining a few rudimentary skills would be so much fun? And so intense?

The awareness between them was like a storm circling. The electricity crackled around them.

It was in their eyes meeting and in the accidental brushing of their hands. It was in *everything.*

And yet, he would not allow himself to follow it. He was always the one who pulled back, reminding himself, sternly, that she was here under his protection and that she was as vulnerable as she had been after her fiancé had left her.

He could not take advantage of that.

It was Angie who reminded him they had a house to get ready for a photo shoot.

And somehow, doing that, was also a journey in discovery.

A few days later, Jefferson watched as Angie settled back into the deepness of the couch and sighed with contentment. The house was nearly ready. They were sitting outside on his deck in the comfort of his living room furniture. It was the last big job they needed to do, get the furniture out. She had insisted on spending a very hot afternoon scrubbing the floors and waxing them.

Now, as they waited for them to dry, the sun

was going down. Jefferson, without asking, had placed a glass of wine in her hand.

"I should have thought of this before," Jefferson said, looking out over the lake. "This furniture is great out here. Very comfortable. I think I'll leave it out here."

They were sprawled out on the sofa. He was covered in sweat, and so was she.

As far as romantic moments went, moving furniture was probably way down the scale. But honestly? If you wanted a woman to see your muscles? Woo-hoo.

"You will not leave it out here," she said. "You'd wreck it."

"Who cares? I barely use it anyway."

"Don't you like it?"

He was silent.

"You don't like it."

"Hailey picked everything for this house."

"Ah, so it has sentimental value."

"The funny thing? I don't think she much liked it, either."

"But why, then?"

"It's a long story." He did not feel ready to tell

it. For when he told her the truth about his marriage, all this magic between them would dissipate. She would see who he really was, that there was nothing remotely heroic about him. But for now, he was not strong enough to break the enchantment between them.

"I think I can hook up the TV to work out here," he said. "You want to watch *Wreck and Me*?"

"Yes!"

And so, as the stars winked on in a glorious night sky, they sat on his couch outside and watched the movie about a solitary ogre who reluctantly falls in love.

Jefferson found himself frowning. That ogre, living alone in his cave, enjoying his life of solitude, reminded him of someone. The beautiful princess, who so desperately needed the reluctant ogre's help, reminded him of someone, too.

He had refilled her wineglass several times, and when the final song, "A Night for Us," came on, it made her bold.

"Dance with me," she whispered. "There's

nothing in the living room. The wax is dry. It makes for a perfect dance floor."

"I'm not much of a dancer." He had to stop this nonsense before he created a problem worse than the one she was running from.

"I love to dance," she said.

"Did you dance with him? With your fiancé?"

She smiled, a touch wryly. "No. He *hated* dancing. I don't think we ever danced together. Once, I bought tickets to a ball. They were very expensive. He said he would go, but then he was conveniently ill that night."

Jefferson contemplated that. If you loved a woman and you knew she liked something, was it not part of what you had signed up for—to put yourself out a bit?

"What did you love about him?" he asked. He wished he could take the words back. Why did he want to know?

She sighed and took the last sip of her wine. "Looking back on it now? It's more like I selected a candidate than fell in love."

"Selected a candidate?"

"I wanted the things I lost when my father

abandoned our family. I wanted to feel secure and safe. Now, I'm not so sure what that has to do with love."

Jefferson felt a shiver along his spine. Why would she know more about love now than she had then?

"It seems to me," she said softly, "maybe love is a leap into the unknown rather than retreat into the known."

This was not going well, Jefferson thought. He was sitting out on his deck on a star-studded night, discussing love with a beautiful, beautiful woman.

The well-known female vocalist's voice soared out over the lake. It seemed to mingle with the stars and the warmth of the summer breeze.

"'We have come through every valley, we have come through every plight,

"'Let me take your hand and show you the magic of the night...'"

Jefferson did the worst possible thing. He needed to avoid this discussion. At the same time he felt a deep, masculine desire to show her he was a better man than Harry.

In his haste to do both, he held out his hand to her. He said to her, his voice a hoarse whisper, "Let's dance."

He realized, too late, he had just taken that great leap into the unknown.

CHAPTER THIRTEEN

ANGIE DID THE worst possible thing. Even though she had instigated this, even though she knew Jefferson had asked her to dance because he felt sorry for her that Harry had been such a boob on the subject, even though she knew it was moving them toward uncharted territory, she put her hand in Jefferson's.

She let him lead her into the house. With the doors of the living room folded open to the night, they swayed together to the hopelessly romantic music. She gazed upon the face she had become so fond of and contemplated what she had revealed, not just to Jefferson, but to herself, about the nature of her and Harry's relationship.

She hadn't loved Harry. She had picked him as the most likely to give her the life she had wanted ever since her father had walked out the door with hardly a glance back.

She knew that now. She had not known it then.

She thought about why she knew it now when she had not known it then. Because now she had eaten ice cream during a storm. Now she had chased a man with a spider, the air ringing with their laughter. Now, she had stood under a waterfall. And squealed as a slippery fish had landed in their boat. Now she had watched *Wreck and Me* under the stars.

Now, she was dancing in an empty room with no one watching.

She stared up at Jefferson and drank in the face that had become so familiar to her. She felt the heat of his body and the strength of it where it was pressed into her.

It occurred to Angie exactly why she knew now that she had not fallen in love with Harry when she had not known it before, even when he left her.

She stopped dancing.

Jefferson stopped dancing.

"Would you like to come to a real dance with

me?" he asked. "The town is having a fund-raiser in Hailey's memory."

She knew it would be craziness to say yes.

"It's going to be very hard for me to go alone."

Which made it impossible to say no.

"It's called A Black Tie Affair."

There was her excuse. She did not have a single thing to wear to a function called A Black Tie Affair.

She started to say it and then snapped her mouth shut.

That was the Angie she had been, before. Before she had driven down that long and winding road and knocked on the door that had led her to this man. To Jefferson.

That was the Angie who had been afraid of everything. Even before she had been stalked she had played it safe, tried to arrange a life that would make her feel comfortable and secure.

Playing it safe, she realized, had not gotten her one single thing that she wanted. The exact opposite was probably true.

"I'd love to go to the dance with you," she said.

"It's on Saturday."

"What day is it today?"

"I have to think about it," he said wryly. "I've lost track of time. Tuesday. Today's Tuesday."

She broke away from him. "That's only four days away. And the photographer from the magazine is coming on Monday. I have a great deal to do."

Not being swayed by the bemusement in his eyes, she fled from Jefferson and went up the stairs to her room.

She knew she should say no to going to the dance, but she could not. She sat down and did a sketch, and stared at it.

It was even more beautiful than the wedding dress she had designed. It had a strap over one shoulder, the other shoulder bare. The upper portion of the dress, bodice to waist, was fitted. And then it flared out in a cloud of whimsy. She had only a few days.

It occurred to her she really did only have a few days. It had been their agreement that she would leave after the photographer came. Her job here would be done. Her time here.

But she felt as she had lying on the sun-warmed stone by the waterfall.

I want to stay here forever.

She reminded herself that Jefferson had broken that spell. That Jefferson broke all the spells. She wanted things to deepen between them. He did not.

And that was good. It was a good thing that one of them could be pragmatic when the storm was building all around them, threatening to pull them right into its vortex of power.

She looked at the dress again. If ever a dress could challenge a man's best intentions, it would be this one. Is that what she wanted to do?

It was what she wanted to do. She did not want to be safe anymore. She wanted to fling herself into the storm, to put herself at the mercy of love.

Love.

She looked at her drawing again and let that word wash over her, felt the power of the feeling that accompanied it. Could she really pull this off?

She thought with longing of the woman she had been, ever so briefly, when that storm was over.

Fearless.

She wanted that again. She wanted to be fearless.

What about getting his house ready for the photographers? She was going to have to do both. She was going to have to be fearless and pragmatic.

Well, anyone who could coax cookies and a sewing project out of thirty reluctant teenagers could most certainly handle the pragmatic aspects of the assignment she had given herself.

She got up from her desk. She went over to those cubbies filled with fabric and sorted through them. They were swatches. It was almost as if they had been put here for show—to add splashes of bright color to the room—rather than to be of use. Angie had managed to scavenge her bathing suit cover from these, but the dress in the sketch was another matter.

She went to the window and stared out at the darkened lake. The breeze lifted a curtain and it caught her eye.

Angie laughed out loud. It was pure white silk. She caressed it with her fingers. She couldn't use his curtains for a dress, could she?

The old Angie might not have been able to. The new Angie got on a chair and tugged the draperies down off their hooks.

Jefferson would not admit how much he missed Angie. Since that night they had danced in the living room, and in a moment of weakness when he had wanted to give her everything she wanted, and had invited her to a real dance, he had barely seen her.

She was a flurry of motion—racing through the house, cleaning crazily, organizing for the photo shoot and then disappearing up the stairs to her room.

She was making meals—in the middle of the night?—and leaving him notes on how to cook them, but he missed her. He was glad they were going to have a whole evening together to just enjoy each other.

On Saturday evening, he came out of his room. He and Hailey had often gone to events that required this kind of garb—the opera, plays, fund-raising balls. He had not dressed like this for a long time. He had never felt like this about it, either. Strangely awkward, almost shy. Standing in the hall, he put a finger between his collar and his neck, trying for a bit of breathing space.

He heard a sound on the stairs that led to Angie's room.

He turned slowly. He dropped his finger from his collar. It was hopeless. He was never going to be able to breathe. Every thought of the impression he was going to make on her fled him as the sight of her—the impression she was making on him—filled his every sense and stole his breath away.

Could this woman be Angie?

Even in that ultra-sexy bathing suit, he had never seen her look like this.

She floated down the staircase toward him on a cloud of white. The dress hugged her upper body, showed the sensuous curve of her recently sun kissed shoulders, then flared out, sweeping around her. She looked like a princess in a fairy tale.

"What?" she asked, pausing on the stairs.

Could she not know what a vision she was?

"Where on earth did that dress come from?" he managed to choke out when that was not what he wanted to say at all. "I'm pretty sure the Emporium does not stock anything like that."

"Have you ever seen *The Sound of Music*?"

"Uh, yeah."

"Curtains," she said. "I'm afraid I owe you a set of curtains."

He vaguely recalled a scene in that movie where curtains had been transformed into play clothes. It was a movie. They would have had a team of tailors and seamstresses working on that.

"How did you do this?" he asked. Another movie came to mind. Cinderella, where the cleaning girl was transformed.

As if drawn to her by an invisible cord, he went and stood before her, looking up the stairs at her, at the sweep of the dress, the delicacy of her naked shoulder, the formfitting bodice.

"This is what I always wanted to do," she said. "I wanted to design clothes."

"And you didn't, why?" He could hear the astonishment in his own voice.

"Because I was told to pick a practical career, and that's what I did. Instead of following my own heart."

She was looking at him with an unnerving intensity, as if that was all changed now. As if she fully intended to follow her own heart from now on.

He realized it was not the dress, alone, that made her beautiful. He realized it was her radiance. He had invited her to go to the dance as a gift to her, to give her something she had always wanted.

Jefferson contemplated the nature of gifts.

For this one had come back to him. It felt as if what he had given her since she arrived, the gift of sanctuary, had unveiled her bit by bit.

Now she stood before him, confident and radiant, the woman she really was, the woman she had always been meant to be.

And so the gift was returned to him. In leading her back to herself, it was he who had come fully alive. This gift of awareness did not fall gently against him. No, it smashed into him with all the force that was needed to take what was left of the severely compromised armor he had put around his heart and leave it in shards.

It felt as though he was stepping over that shattered armor as he reached for her, as her hand came into his, as he placed his kiss of recognition and welcome first on the top of her hand and then on her cheek.

He could fight no more.

They went by boat to Anslow. That journey, through inky waters, the spray from the boat white against blackness of the sky and the lake was the beginning of the magic. When they arrived he had to squeeze in to find a place to tie up, there were so many boats at the dock. A horse and carriage were at the end of it, waiting to take guests who had arrived by water to the community hall.

The interior of the hall had been transformed with thousands of bright fairy lights. They illuminated the line of the roof, climbing the walls like vines, tracing the outlines of linen-covered tables.

The place was packed. The people of Anslow loved an occasion—weddings, graduations, fund-raisers—they kept finery that would not have been out of place in New York City for these community events.

There were no speeches, just a dinner followed by a clearing of the tables, a bar being set up, a band taking their places on the raised stage at one end of the room.

He introduced Angie to people who had been his family and his friends and his neighbors since he was six years old.

They welcomed him into the fold of their lives as if he was a soldier who had been away from home for too long. They extended their acceptance of him to Angie. But almost too much so! He could not get near the woman he had escorted to the dance.

She quickly became the belle of the ball. For the first set, every old geezer in Anslow had to claim a dance with her. By the second set, the young men who had been fortifying their courage at the bar were jostling to have a turn around the hall with her.

Angie, amazing in that dress, was an astonishing dancer. Her movements were fluid and natural and unconsciously sensual. Her laughter carried through the hall. Her face was flushed. Her eyes were radiant. She was a princess, casting an enchantment.

Watching her, dance, watching her shine, Jefferson had a sense of having done the right thing. This is what she had led him to again and again since she had arrived at his door.

She required him to do the right thing. She forced him to be a better man.

And then, for the third set, he wearied of all the attention being paid to her and went and claimed her for his own. When Gerry Mack tried to cut in, he told him no. By the time the fourth and final set of the evening arrived, no one was trying to cut in anymore.

They danced until their feet ached. They danced until they could hardly breathe. They danced until the last dance, when he held her tight, rested his chin on the top of her head and realized something had happened that he thought would never happen again.

He was happy.

The evening broke up, and the poor old horse and carriage could not keep up with people flocking down to the dock, so he and Angie walked along the boardwalk, hand in hand. The night was filled with the laughter and chatter of the crowds. They were not the only ones walking.

As they turned at the entrance of the dock, a flurry of farewells filled the air.

"So good to see you, Jefferson. Angie, nice to meet you."

"Safe journey over the water, Jeff. Angie, thank you for coming."

Finally, he helped her into the boat and settled her in her seat. He went and got the blanket from below and tucked it over her shoulders.

"They love you," Angie said, tugging the blanket around herself. She was glowing.

He contemplated her words. How right it seemed for the word *love* to have floated into the enchantment that was tonight.

He started the engine, put on the running

lights, backed away from the dock and pointed the nose of his boat toward the dark main body of water of Kootenay Lake. Driving at night was extraordinarily beautiful, but it held some extra challenges.

"Jefferson?"

He turned his focus from the water, looked at her.

"They love you. And so do I."

For the second time that night, it felt as if his breath had quit and his heart had stopped. What was he doing? Hadn't he known all along this is where it was going?

"They only think they love me," he told her. "And so do you."

"No," she said stubbornly.

Rather than respond, he checked for other boats leaving the harbor and, seeing none, opened up the throttle. Everybody only thought they loved him. If only they knew how unworthy he was.

He realized he could give the boat all the gas he wanted, but he could not go fast enough to outrun what had to be done.

He had to tell her. He had to put this to a stop right now, before he undid every bit of good the past two weeks had done for her.

He didn't respond to her at first. He drove them over the quiet lake—so much of it now held memories of their times together—and pulled into the cove where they had taken refuge from the storm. He stopped the boat and put out the anchor.

The boat rocked gently. The night air was as warm as an embrace. He could still hear voices and laughter drifting over the lake. Angie sat looking at him, the dress a dream around her, so beautiful it made him ache.

"It is a perfect night," she said. "Or would be if I had ice cream."

It had been. It had been a perfect night. But it wasn't going to be anymore. Because every good memory he had of this night would be overridden by what was going to happen next. This was the night it was all going to end.

"I have to tell you something," Jefferson said quietly.

CHAPTER FOURTEEN

I HAVE TO tell you something.

It seemed to Angie as if every horrible event of her whole life had begun with those words.

Her mother looking at her with red, swollen eyes, her voice broken. "I have to tell you something. Your father and I are getting divorced. He moved out this morning."

Harry, biting his lip and then looking away, before clearing his throat and saying in a firm voice, "I have to tell you something. It's not good news, I'm afraid. I'm not happy. I can't be happy here. I've met someone."

Her father had met someone, too, not that she had known it at the time. If she had known, maybe she could have been more prepared for how her life was about to change.

And then Harry turned out to be exactly like her father, as if she could spot a philanderer across a crowded room, when what she was looking for was the exact opposite.

So, what did Jefferson have to tell her? Selfishly, she wished he would wait until morning. She did not want to end what had been one of the nicest nights of her life on a sour note! How cruel of him to park the boat in the middle of a lake where she had no option to run and hide once he had told her.

But that's what she got for declaring her love. That's what she got for being fearless when she was the person least inclined that way. Why hadn't she just accepted who she was instead of pushing her boundaries?

"I had no right to enjoy tonight as much as I did," Jefferson announced quietly.

She felt suddenly panicky. "You can spare me the details," she said. "I think I can guess. You have a girlfriend tucked away somewhere, don't you? I should have known, really. A man like you—so gorgeous and so much fun and so successful—could not possibly be alone for so long. I—"

"Angie. Stop it! Of course I don't have a girl-friend."

Her relief was short-lived. "A horrible ail-ment," she decided. "Are you dying?"

"No. Angie, just let me speak. Please."

"I'm trapped on a boat. What choice do I have?" How could she have been so dumb? How could she have declared her love for him? Now, he had to make excuses. She braced her-self for it. She could imagine what was coming. He didn't love her. He was going to try and let her down gently. *I like you very much. I hope we can remain friends.*

"Are you listening?" he asked.

"No, I'm contemplating jumping off the boat. Unfortunately, the weight of the dress, wet, would probably drown me."

"As if I would ever let you drown," he said, annoyed.

That made her look at him. There was a pro-tective fury in his voice. And there was some-thing tortured in the way he was looking at her.

"Okay," she said, taking a deep breath, "I'm listening."

"Those people, who you so correctly pointed out love me, are trying to help me. They were so insistent I come tonight, because they are trying to bring me back to their world. But I feel their love is with an illusion, because they have no idea who I really am."

She stared at him. He was standing at the back of the boat, his weight rocking easily from foot to foot with the boat's motion. How could he believe people had no idea who he was when he radiated who he was?

All that quiet confidence and strength.

"Everybody is trying to make me feel better about what happened that night with Hailey. They're trying to make me feel better, they want me to get on with my life. But I would have to absolve myself, and I can't."

"Absolve yourself?" she whispered.

"Here's the truth no one knows," he said harshly. "Here's the truth you need to know before you make your declaration of love.

"We fought that night. That's what sent her out onto those terrible roads. We had had a terrible fight. And I was so mad, I didn't go after her. I knew she didn't know those roads. I failed her. I failed to protect her. Isn't that what I swore I would do, when I said those vows to her?"

"Jefferson, what happened?"

He looked out over the lake, pensive. When he spoke again, his voice was quiet. Angie had to strain to hear it.

"I could not believe my ears when Hailey said she wanted to build a house on the land I'd inherited from my grandparents. My grandparents' house had already burned down by the time I met her, so our trips to the property were not exactly successes. We tried camping once. That was a disaster. We stayed at the hotel in Anslow twice, and that didn't meet her standards.

"That's nothing against her—she was a big-city girl, with a high-powered career that was just reaching its pinnacle. I knew that when I married her.

"I was fine with our life. I loved my wife. We had a swanky apartment in downtown Vancouver. Both of us traveled a lot with our careers. When we were together it was fancy dinners and theater and entertaining friends. I was content with all of that.

"Until she said she wanted to build a house here, on my land, on Kootenay Lake. And then I knew how much I had missed it and how much I wanted to come home. Then, I knew I harbored other dreams beyond the amazing success I was enjoying. Of having a family, and of campfires on summer nights and long days on the boat.

"We started building in the spring. It was a huge undertaking. Summer was the best part of the whole project. We lived in a holiday trailer, but everything seemed exciting—things were happening, the house was taking shape. We'd work all day, then swim and sit around a little campfire roasting hot dogs.

"But, right from the start, there were disagreements. She picked an impractical location for the house because it would "showcase" her skills. The whole project very quickly seemed to become about showcasing her skills. Budget went out the window with the building of the road to the house site, and it went downhill from there.

"Double ovens in the kitchen? She didn't even

cook. A craft room? You could not meet a person less interested in being crafty than Hailey.

"Then the build went into the fall. It was wet and grim. By the time we finished and moved in, Hailey hated it here. It's cold that close to the water. It's foggy. Because of where she chose to put the house, it was incredibly difficult to get in and out of it.

"But, finally, we were nearing completion. That's when she started picking furniture. Every single thing seemed to be about how it looked instead of how it felt.

"And that night when we fought, she was placing furniture and it slipped out that she was staging the house. Staging. That's what you do to manipulate people's impressions of a space—it's like you're creating a fantasy they can walk into. It's not what you do if you're planning on living there.

"So, I pressed her on that, what she meant by staging, and she admitted all of it had really been with an eye to a future sale. The property, by itself, is probably worth millions. With the house on it?

"She figured with the proceeds of this sale we could buy a piece of property in any big city in the world that we wanted, and she could build our *real* house there. Our real house, the house for the busy professional couple, with no children. She actually laughed when I asked her where our kids fit into the picture.

"I'm not proud of what happened next. I lost my mind. I started smashing all her little staging items—her expensive vases and her pictures that didn't mean anything to anybody. I'm not sure I have ever been so angry.

"And she left. She left in the middle of a snowstorm and drove away. And I didn't go after her.

"No, I sat and brooded over the mistake I'd made, and asked myself how I couldn't have seen sooner what was coming. I didn't think—not once—about all the things I loved about her. The way she laughed, and how smart she was, and how she liked to play jokes on me. I didn't think about all the good years we'd had before we started to build that house, or all the things we had in common. No, I got rip-roaring drunk, and I passed out on the couch.

"I woke up to a knock at the door. It was the police. She'd made it up our road to the highway. But she had tried to take a corner too fast. It was slippery. She'd gone off the road. She died on impact, when the car hit the water."

Angie could feel the tears streaming down her face. She got up from where she had been sitting and stood behind him. She wrapped her arms around him and leaned her head into his back.

He jerked away from her. He spun and looked at her. His eyes were dark with a fury that made her take a step back from him, even though it was obvious the fury was directed at himself.

"That's the me that nobody knows," he said grimly. "I killed her. She had nowhere to go when I got mad like that. I might as well have put a gun to her head and pulled the trigger."

Angie gasped at that, but he wasn't done.

"You were right. Those people love me. They've loved me since I was a six-year-old boy. But they don't know me. And I don't think they'd be trying so damned hard to make something good come out of something bad if they knew the full truth."

"Jefferson," Angie said, her voice a croak of pure pain, "it was an accident. You did not kill your wife. That is a terrible burden you've been carrying. You are a good man."

He looked at her long and hard. And then he pushed past her and took his seat at the controls of the boat. He flicked it on and gave it full throttle. The nose lifted so quickly, she was thrust into one of the back seats. They shot over the still water like a rocket that had been launched.

When they arrived at his dock and he helped her out of the boat, his face remained grim.

"Don't love me," he said. And then he turned and walked away.

Angie watched him go. It was already too late for that. She already did love him, beyond reason. The fact that he carried this terrible burden of guilt, along with his grief, did not make her love him less.

But it did make her see the truth. Perhaps it was the truth he had already seen.

She was hiding here. Cowering, really, from what life had handed her. To love him, to lead him through everything that love meant she could not cower.

She had to face her life head-on.

She had to show him she did not need his protection. He had set himself up in that role, a role he already thought he had failed at.

And she had allowed it. She had taken great comfort in it.

But it had done what it needed to do. It had helped to heal her. Now, to love him, she had to come to him whole, not in fragments of fear and not a hostage to her own history. She had to dig deep within herself and be the person he had shown her she could be. She had to give him back what he had given her. She had to lend him her strength, just as he had lent her his.

And she could see only one way she could do that.

Angie had to be fearless.

Jefferson went to his room without waiting to see how Angie would react to all he had told her. In the morning, he expected she would look at him with the disdain of someone who had been shown a truth that was different from what they had believed.

He expected he might see signs she had been crying.

Instead, when he ventured out of his room in the morning, he saw Angie was already busy. The muffins were fresh baked, as always. He heard her in the living room.

"The photographer is coming tomorrow," she called to him.

He resisted an impulse to yell he didn't give a damn about the photographer. Was she going to pretend he hadn't said anything last night? He grabbed a muffin and went and stood in the door of the living room.

The princess was gone, and Cinderella was back, her hair hidden under one of her babushka creations, her shorts showing off the slenderness of her legs, her T-shirt clinging. She had a small mountain of pillows on the floor.

"Where did those come from?" he asked gruffly.

"I made them."

How was it possible to like this as much as

the goddess she had been last night? How was it possible to *love* this as much.

Love.

There was that word again. And the truth smashed into him. He loved her. Enough to let her go on to the life she deserved.

"When?" he asked.

"Last night. I couldn't sleep."

So, she was more distressed by what he had told her than she was letting on. He could see that now. She was avoiding looking at him.

He stuffed the entire blueberry muffin in his mouth, as if somehow, that could help him stuff back the terrible sensation of loss that was sweeping through him, even though she was standing right here.

"You need to go see if you can find some flowers," she said, placing a pillow on the couch. She scowled at it, then karate chopped the top of it. "I should have asked to have the ones from the dinner tables last night."

He scowled. He had just laid an earth-shattering truth about himself at her feet, and she was going to talk about flowers?

Well, fine, he'd go along with that. He'd go find some flowers. He didn't want to be around her anyway. It caused an ache in him that felt as if it would never go away.

Grabbing another muffin, he went out the door.

He made sure he was gone a good long time. He emptied Anslow of flowers and then, as an afterthought, he pulled off the lake and picked a bouquet of wildflowers from the hills. The wildflowers, he somehow knew, would delight her more than the ones he had gotten from the tiny flower shop in Anslow.

Why, he asked himself, was he picking wildflowers for her.

Because, at the very core of every man, was a little light that flickered, that would not be put out, not even if you threw pails of water on it.

That light was hope.

But that light died in him when, laden with flowers as she had requested, he went back into his house.

Maybe, subliminally, he had registered that

her car was not parked under the tree where it had been since the day she arrived.

Maybe, subliminally, he had registered there was no movement in the windows, no lights on, as he had come up the staircase from the lake.

Whatever it was, he knew the instant he walked in the door. He knew before he called her name and walked room to room looking for her. He knew before he took the stairs, two at a time, up to her room and found the closets empty and her suitcase gone.

The wildflowers fell from his hand and scattered across the bleached hardwood floor.

He had known before having evidence, because it was as if her essence was gone from the house.

He walked back through, more slowly. It was strange, because the house was as perfect as it had ever been. As he went from room to room, he saw it looked exactly as Hailey had dreamed it would look. Staged, to give the illusion it was someone's home.

There was a throw over the couch, and a wooden apple crate beside it filled with magazines. There was a hardcover book, turned over, open, making it look as if someone had sat here reading and they had just gotten up for a second. The fireplace, that had never been used, was laid for a fire as if it was just waiting for a match.

The kitchen had a platter of cookies on the island and a basket of the small green apples that grew wild on the road down to the house. He knew them to be inedible, but they were a delight to the eye and created that illusion of homeyness. On the counter, there was a cookbook open on a reading rack, and a bottle of wine with two glasses.

She had disobeyed him and gone into his bedroom. There were candles on the bedside tables, and the scent of freshly laundered sheets filled his nostrils. And right underneath that scent was one that reminded him of her. She didn't know that he had saved Hailey's pillow, and he went to it and pressed it to his face.

Hailey's scent was gone from it. And after what he had revealed last night, that seemed fitting.

There was not a nook or corner of his house that had not been cleaned to sparkling. The little details were everywhere, but she was not.

Angie was gone.

And he did not blame her for going. She had fulfilled the letter of her agreement with him. She had refused his further protection, which given his failure to Hailey, was understandable.

Jefferson fought down the feeling of panic rising in him. There was a nut job out there who wanted Angie and who was most likely responsible for the disappearance of another woman.

He scoured his house for a note from her that would leave him a clue to where she was, but he found nothing.

Even though he had brought this on himself, he felt furious with Angie for the impotence he felt. He had known last night's revelations would force her to leave if she was smart, which he knew she was.

But, somehow, he had thought he would engineer the exit plan, so that he could know she was safe. How dare she wake him up—to the point he could feel again—and then leave him with this sense of abject helplessness? Leave him to face his demons: he had failed to protect Hailey, and now he could not protect Angie either.

No doubt, she would go into deeper hiding than ever. She was clever. If she didn't want to be found, he was pretty sure Winston would not find her.

But he wouldn't, either. For his own sanity, he had to know she was all right. How was he going to do that? He was a man with resources. And plenty of them.

Within an hour, he had the most elite private detective agency in the world looking for Angie. Vibrating with tension, needing something to occupy him, he turned his attention to the final stages of getting the house ready for the magazine.

CHAPTER FIFTEEN

ANGIE SAT AT the window of the coffee shop, sipping a cup of tea, waiting. She should have felt nervous. But she didn't. She felt strangely and wonderfully elated.

She had experienced an epiphany that night of A Black Tie Affair, coming home on the boat with Jefferson. He had told her everything about himself, exposed what he perceived as his weaknesses to her. She knew he had been trying to chase her away.

What he had done was the exact opposite. Angie realized she had pursued love for all the wrong reasons for her whole life. She had wanted to feel safe and secure. It had always been all about her.

But what she felt for Jefferson—what had grown over their two weeks together and culminated on his boat that final night—was so much bigger than that.

It made her realize who she had to be to love that man. And that realization made her feel bold and fully alive for the first time in her life. The realization that she loved the man beyond reason required her to fearlessly embrace the unknown, not retreat into safety. It required her to be whole and strong, not to go to Jefferson weak and afraid and filled with neediness.

A voice crackled in her ear. It startled her, but she resisted the urge to reach up to her ear and adjust the tiny bud that had been planted there.

"We have the subject parking his car. He's out. He's coming to the door."

"Okay," she whispered.

Hidden in a brooch she had attached to the lapel of the suit jacket she was wearing was a microphone. She was "wired" just like in the movies.

Angie watched as the door to the restaurant slid open. She felt her heart begin to beat hard. Up until this point, they had not even been sure the message she had left on Winston's Facebook page had reached him or if he would respond to it if it had.

Winston stood there, scanning the room. Angie's sense of confidence evaporated. He was innocent enough looking: an ordinary bespectacled man in a sports jacket and jeans. The bow tie, and blue-checkered shirt, added to the air of benign befuddlement, as if he was a professor trying to figure out which class he was supposed to be in.

But underneath that, when he narrowed his eyes and caught sight of her, Angie saw the truth of him. His gaze was that of a predator who had spotted prey. There was the glint of pure malice before it was masked with a smile. She fought a desire to shudder and, more, to get up and bolt.

She took a deep breath. She reminded herself she was in a crowded room. She reminded herself that the police were right outside, and that they would listen to every word. She reminded herself that this wasn't just about her. Or even about Jefferson. It was about putting away a dangerous man; it was about protecting another unsuspecting woman, or maybe even more than one.

She had, with police help, rehearsed a script. She needed to put Winston at ease enough to talk about the woman who was missing.

Winston sat down across from her. A little smile flickered across his face as he looked at her. What was it? Suspicion? Hope? Slyness?

"Hello, Angie," he said.

She took another deep, steadying breath. She reminded herself of the fearless woman she had been on the deck of that pitching boat. Her lips stretched into what she hoped was a smile of amiable greeting.

"Hello, Winston."

It was a game of cat and mouse, luring him into her confidence. After a few pleasantries, she began to talk about Harry and his new girl-friend. She claimed she had gone away because she needed to think, to recover from Harry's betrayal. She had to manufacture indignation, because these days, she saw Harry as a neces-sary step to being put on the most important road of all. The road to herself.

Once she had talked about Harry, it was an easy enough thing to turn the talk to Winston's ex, to follow a carefully crafted script that led him deeper and deeper down a road he could not retreat from.

As his barriers dropped, Angie had the chilling feeling Winston *wanted* her to know what had happened to his ex. That he was pleased with himself. That he wanted her to know what he was capable of, so that he could use it to control her.

He told her everything. He trusted her. He incriminated himself. He, no doubt, thought that even if she wasn't so frightened she would never speak of this again, no one would ever believe her if she repeated this chilling tale.

"Good job. We've got him," the voice said in her ear. "Tell him you have to leave now."

She looked at her watch. "Oh! Look at the time. I have to go, Winston. It's been nice catching up."

He looked stunned at this easy dismissal. And then he looked angry. He was seething as he followed her to the cashier.

"I'll get it," he snapped, when she reached for her purse.

But the thought of his money paying for one thing she had ingested nauseated her. She shook her head. She was pretty sure he noticed her hand trembling as she passed the bills to the cashier.

"When am I going to see you again?" he demanded.

"I'm just not sure."

He stared at her. "There's someone else," he said. "Isn't there?"

She was not safe yet. She edged toward the door.

"I can see it in your face," he said. And then he sighed with what might have seemed like defeat if she was not so wary of him. "I'd like to give you something. To remember me by."

She was sure that was true.

"Just walk out to my car with me."

She had no doubt he would love her to accompany him to his car, that he would look for an opportunity to overwhelm her.

"Sure," she said, and went out the door. He

was gloating over her acceptance. She had rehearsed this part with the police, too. Get out the door. Go instantly right. A policeman grabbed her and pulled her out of the way.

Winston, still gloating over the fact she had agreed to accompany him to his car, did not even see it coming. He was on the ground in a sea of blue in the blink of an eye. Then he was yanked to his feet.

Panting, he pulled against the arms that held him, glaring at her, radiating pure malevolence. "I'll get you, you bitch," he promised.

Angie stared at him. And then she actually threw back her head and laughed. "Don't you get it? I got you. Your game is over."

And then, feeling as free and as fearless as she had ever felt in her life, she turned and walked away.

Now, she was worthy to love Jefferson.

Jefferson's phone rang. He snatched it out of his pocket and felt a whoosh of pure relief at the number on the screen. He had been waiting for this call for three days.

He had not been able to work. Or sleep. Or eat. The photographers had come and gone with him hardly noticing their presence. He was not sure if he had ever experienced the sense of helplessness that had gripped him over the past few days.

"Have you found her?" he demanded.

"Yes, we've located her."

"Is she safe?"

"Oh, yeah."

Jefferson felt as if he had been holding his breath and was finally allowed to breathe. He was not sure what to make of the cavalier tone in the PI's voice.

"What do you mean by that?" he asked.

"She's more than fine. Angelica Witherspoon is quite the woman."

"Excuse me?"

"I tracked her down through a source at the Calgary Police Service. She was at the center of a sting. They got that bastard. Because of her."

"Huh?"

"My source says he's been doing police work for twenty-two years and has never seen anyone perform like that. She was so calm and cool, and confident. She walked him right into a trap. He'll never breathe another free breath."

"She did what?" Jefferson sputtered. "We're talking about Angie? Angelica Witherspoon?"

His detective repeated the whole story with great relish and more detail.

Jefferson tried to make this line up with the woman who had arrived at his door four weeks ago.

He couldn't make it happen.

But as he thought of who she had become over their two weeks together, he knew what he was hearing was true.

She was braver than he had ever believed. And she was stronger than she had ever believed.

Still, when he hung up the phone, what he felt was an abject sense of loss. He felt the desolation of a man who had somehow touched heaven and was being sent back to earth.

Her foolhardiness only reminded him of what he already knew. Life was capricious. Things had turned out well, but they could have just as easily gone the other way. He could have gotten a phone call that reminded him, again, of his impotency. Of his failure to protect.

His phone rang again.

He saw Angelica Witherspoon flash across the screen. He wanted to talk to her more than he had ever wanted anything in his life. He wanted to scream at her for her foolishness and tell her to come home.

Home.

The place that both held hope and dashed hope. The place that tantalized with a vision of love, and then could take it all away.

He didn't answer her call. And when he listened to her message and heard her words, he was so glad he had not.

I love you.

He clicked it off without listening to the rest of the message. She loved the one who could not protect her. Had he heard her speak those words, his every strength would have fled him. He would have begged her to come and fill this empty void his life had become.

Instead, he turned off his phone and tucked it away. He would get about the very serious business of proving to himself and to her he could go on without her.

It felt like a mission as he made his way to the kitchen, opened the freezer, remembered some particularly wonderful thing she had done with chicken breast. He had seen in her eyes, that first day, when she had looked at his tinned collection of food, that she had felt pity for him.

And one thing about Jefferson Stone? He despised pity. He had been on the receiving end of too much for his entire life. His parents. His grandparents. Hailey. He was not going to be the object of anyone's pity, ever again.

He probably had some kind of curse on him. The curse of loss.

His resolve to stand on his own, to not ever invite anyone else into his wretched life, firmed. If he truly wanted chicken dinner and muffins, he was quite capable of doing that for himself. He did not *need* Angie Witherspoon aka Brook Nelson. He did not *need* anyone. It was safest that way.

He returned to his office, but only to pick up his electronic tablet. He put what he needed into the search engine, and snorted to himself at how ridiculously easy it was to cook a rosemary chicken breast. Buoyed by that success, he also looked up muffins.

It occurred to him that he didn't know where the mixing bowls were or even if he had any. Wasn't it high time he found out?

Whistling with grim determination—and not Jingle Bells, either—Jefferson renewed his vow of complete independence. He found the bowls and some rudimentary ingredients. He began to slap things together.

Angie set down the phone. Jefferson had not answered. She felt the first real fear she had felt since she had returned to snare Winston. She looked at her watch. She could be back at the Stone House in a matter of hours.

But what if he didn't want to see her? What if it was over between them? What if she could not restore his faith in himself?

This, she told herself, was not the time to allow her courage to fail her.

She made the trip in what she imagined was

record time. She was surprised she had not gotten a speeding ticket.

Now, she stood outside that door where she had stood just a few weeks ago, when she was a totally different person. She took a deep breath, and she gripped the knocker firmly in her hand.

She could hear him coming.

The door swung open.

She stared at Jefferson.

Oh, beloved, she thought to herself. He had regressed. His shirt was rumpled, and his hair was uncombed. He didn't look as though his face has seen a razor since she had left. He looked utterly exhausted.

She loved him more than she had ever loved him, more even, than that night of enchantment when he had been dressed so beautifully in a formal suit, and she in a gown suited to a princess.

"Nope," he said.

It was hardly the declaration of undying love she had hoped for after her absence!

He started to close the door, but not as firmly as he would have if he really did not want to see her. Come to that, if he really didn't want to see her, he wouldn't have even come to the door.

She stuck her foot in it before he managed to get it closed all the way.

He reopened it and glared at her foot, before lifting his eyes to hers. There were walls up that a less determined person—a less courageous person—might not be able to scale.

"Are you burning the house down?" she asked. "Because it smells as if you are."

"What's it to you? You didn't even leave a note."

She saw the hurt in him before he quickly masked it with a scowl. "Yes, I did. I left it right on the kitchen counter where you would be sure to see it."

"There was no note. What did you say in it? That you were going to single-handedly apprehend a very dangerous person?"

"How did you know that?" she asked.

He glared at her.

"It wasn't single-handed," she said. "I had an entire police team working with me. Jefferson, something is burning. Could we—"

He turned from her, and she followed him through the living room to the kitchen.

It was a shambles.

"No wonder you couldn't find the note," she said.

"It didn't look like this, then."

Black smoke was pouring out of his oven.

"Hell's bells," he snapped.

She was not sure how it was possible the room could be in worse shape than the day she had first seen it, The overhead lights were on, shining an unforgiving light on the disaster and illuminating the thin wisps of smoke that layered the air despite windows opened wide.

Gooey bowls were over on their sides. The countertops dripped mysterious substances onto the floors. A muffin tin—which looked suspiciously as if it was filled with partially cooked muffins—was upside down on the island.

And Jefferson Stone stood, with his back to her, cursing. His hair was silky and just a little too long, and it touched the collar of that same rumpled denim shirt. The shirt showed off the incredible breadth of his shoulders and how the wideness of his back tapered to narrowness at his waist. The untucked shirttails, thankfully, covered most of the enticing curve of his bottom but clung to strength of his legs, set wide. His feet were still sexily bare.

Angie felt an almost animal awareness of how beautifully he was made, how mouthwateringly masculine he was. It made the mess all around him fade.

He turned from the oven to her. She hoped it wasn't the little gasp of pure weakness that rose in her throat and escaped past her lips, like a sigh of longing, that turned him.

He swung around to her, and her sense of being too aware of how beautifully he was made, intensified. The shadow of whiskers on his cheeks and chin had darkened even more. His features were honed and masculine and perfect.

She knew she had been traveling, and her appearance was probably disheveled. She had been so eager to see him she had not even stopped to run a comb through her hair or dab a bit of lipstick on her lips. She put a hand to her tangled hair. His eyes followed her hand, his gaze so dark and direct it sent a delighted shiver up and down her spine.

Stop it, she ordered herself. They had things to say to each other. Or at least, she had things to say to him. But the awareness that hissed in the air between them, like static, like the coming of a storm, was distracting.

A blackened, smoldering chunk of something was dangling from a fork in his hand.

"Is that on fire?" she asked, dragging her eyes away from the piercing gray-blue of his eyes to the welcome distraction of what he held in his hand.

He looked down at the chicken breast, turned quickly and tossed it into the sink before swiveling back to her. "Of course not."

She sniffed the air and raised an eyebrow at him.

He frowned. "Smoldering."

"Ah."

"Prefire, at best."

"Of course."

"The smoke detectors didn't even go off."

"Maybe they aren't working properly," she said, and that earned her a scowl. "Have you tested them recently?"

He was silent.

"I'll add it to my list of things to do," she decided out loud.

"Your things to do?" he sputtered.

"How did the photo shoot go?"

"Swimmingly," he bit out.

She hazarded a few steps in, stopped at the kitchen island and lifted the upside-down muffin tin with cautious fingers. Gluey strings tried to hold it to the counter top, but she succeeded at flipping it over. She stared down. The openings were filled with half-cooked batter that had evidently risen over the confines of the wells provided for them.

"What on earth were you trying to accomplish?" she finally managed to ask him, lifting her eyes to his.

"I had a sudden inexplicable need to lower my sodium intake," he said, crossing his arms defensively over his chest and glaring at her as if this was all her fault.

"I'm sorry. I'm sorry I went away."

He lifted a shoulder as if he didn't care. "You can go away again," he said, his voice hoarse, his posture so stiff it looked as though the tiniest nudge would break him in two. "Clearly, I don't need you."

"Clearly," she agreed softly.

He glared at her with suspicion. He nodded at his mess as if it were a success. "Your presence is unnecessary," he said, lifting his chin in defiance of the wreckage all around him. "I am quite capable of looking after myself."

"Yes," she said soothingly. "Yes. I can clearly see—"

A terrible little giggle escaped her. She tried to stifle it by putting her fist to her lips. It didn't work.

"I wanted the chicken like that. Blackened."

She swallowed hard and spoke over her fist. "Of...course...you...did." Between the words were the strangled remnants of suppressed laughter. She really had said quite enough, but she felt compelled to add, "And the desire to cook...muffins came from?"

"Men," he informed her proudly, "are extremely suggestible animals, particularly when it comes to food. I wanted a muffin, I saw no reason I should not make one for myself."

"A statement of independence," she said.

He looked annoyed at her deduction.

Laughter. It had become, until a few weeks ago, as foreign to her as a forgotten language. Her life had been so strained. She had lived with the extreme tension of feeling hunted and not safe. All that had changed. Her laughter died when she realized that Jefferson was not in any way, shape or form sharing her enjoyment. In fact, Jefferson Stone looked downright grim.

"I wasn't laughing at you," she said, contrite. "It's just that it feels so good to be here. And so right."

Jefferson frowned at that. In case she mistook his silence as an invitation to exchange confidences, he looked long and hard at her, and then gave his head a shake. "I can't see how this is possibly going to work," he muttered.

"We could give it a free trial," she suggested softly.

"I already told you. I don't need you."

"If you decide it's not what you want, I'll refund your misery."

"I told you," he said, "I don't need you."

"What if it's not about need, Jefferson? What if it's not about what either of us needs?"

He didn't say anything.

"What if it's about want? About wanting a different kind of life, not needing it?"

He looked unimpressed. How he reminded her of the man who had first stood in his doorway, arms folded over his chest, his one word—*nope*—hanging between them.

She hadn't let his attitude stop her then, and she wasn't going to let it stop her now. Just like then, it felt as if her life depended on changing that nope to something else. "Can I tell you what I see?"

"Please don't," he said, his voice hard and cold.

She smiled, because she had already seen beyond that mask. She had already seen the strength and the decency that were at his very core.

"I see a man," she said quietly and firmly,

"who despite his dizzying career and financial success, lives with an abject sense of failure. I see a man who viewed himself as helpless when it counted the most, when he most wanted to be powerful.

"I see a man who has suffered way too much loss, and all that loss has left him feeling guarded about love, unwilling to risk such terrifying powerlessness and loss again.

"I see a man who doesn't *need* love but who wants it desperately. And yet he'll say no to that—to rediscovering the richness of his emotional life, to learning to laugh again—because the risk of pain seems like too great a risk."

"It is. Too. Great. A. Risk. And I don't want to talk to you about risks. How could you have done that? Put yourself in the path of that psychopath?"

"I had to."

"But why?"

"Because I was like the Cowardly Lion, I had to find my courage."

He snorted.

"Because there is no love without courage. To

choose love? Even though it has wounded you? That is the greatest courage of all."

Angie heard the firmness in her voice, the new strength of a woman who had found the courage to face down her own fears—all of them. "It's the only risk worth taking. The tremendous payoff is worth the risk. The payoff is love."

When Angie had laughed he had known the gig was up. The minute he had let her in that door, all those weeks ago, he had opened up a whole world of danger to himself.

Her laughter had shown him, all too clearly, who she really was.

And who she really was? Vivacious and fun, alight with life. Smart. Capable. And now this added element: pure, unadulterated courage. What could be more dangerous to his shut-down world than someone like her who was willing to grow and change, to let life teach her all its lessons, both easy and hard? What could be more threatening to the comforting darkness he had come to live in, than her promise of light?

Still, he tried. He cleared his throat.

"Let's look at the facts," he said.

She wrinkled her nose at him. He *hated* it that she did that. It made her look so adorably cute.

He cleared his throat. She had been back in his house less than three minutes and he was already *reacting* to her.

"That moment of madness when I decided I was capable of making muffins?"

"You totally miss me," she said.

He scowled at her. "It is the result of your intrusion on my world, influencing me, filling me with a desire to prove things that did not need proving a mere month ago!"

He had thought, when she had first arrived, that it was only for two weeks. That was all. He'd been clear about that. A man could handle anything for two short weeks.

She moved toward him. He had plenty of opportunity to move away. Plenty. But he did not.

She came and stood before him. Everything she was, was before him. It was in her eyes, sparkling with unshed tears, and in her posture and in her exquisitely beautiful but tentative smile. She was courage and she was delicacy. She was strength and she was tenderness. She was tears and she was laughter.

She was offering him a world that would go from black-and-white to full color; she was offering him a world that would go from bleak to glorious. All of that was in her as she reached out her hand and cupped his jawline, her fingers stretching out to touch his cheekbones.

He froze. He could feel the utter tenderness of her touch. In her shining eyes was love and acceptance. He understood every man dreams of such a thing, without knowing that it was his greatest longing.

Jefferson Stone's strength completely failed him, crumbled like rock from an ancient wall.

Or maybe that was not it. Maybe that was not it at all. Maybe it was that his strength was replaced with the courage she had talked about. And that courage unfurled within him like a flag that had felt the wind.

The wind was her love, showing him all that he could be and all that they could be and all that their world could be.

Because, instead of moving away from the promise of her touch, he moved toward it. He covered her hand with his, and then he guided her hand to his mouth and kissed her fingertips with the reverence of recognition.

Of who this amazing woman was and what she was offering him.

She felt his moment of surrender. Her eyes widened, and the tears were finally freed. Her mouth formed the most delectable little O. And then she was crying, and laughing at the same time.

He gathered her in his arms and felt the pure homecoming of his heart finding its way back. He whispered his thanks to her and to the universe and to whatever forces had guided them toward this moment.

This exquisite moment, when all the world stopped, when every other single thing fell away in insignificance, when all the world bowed before the glory of it.

When all the world acknowledged that there really was only one truth.

And that one truth was love.

EPILOGUE

JEFFERSON STONE WENT and stood at the window for a moment. The moody waters of the main body of the lake were swathed in the chill gray cloud of winter, but the water at the edges of the sheltered bays was freezing up nicely.

The wind howled under the eaves of the house and tossed pebbles of slanting snow against the window. Here, inside, the contrast was sharp and delicious. The house was warm and cozy. He could smell pumpkin pie cooking. December would not be everyone's favorite time to be on the lake, but it was his.

Had December always been his favorite month, with its mercurial weather changes, and with skating on the lake and Christmas right around the corner? Probably it had not been. Once, he had wandered away, like a man lost, from the magic of all those things.

He and Angie had married on Christmas Day. He had offered her the big spring wedding, knowing that dream had been yanked from her once without warning.

But Angie had said no, that wasn't her dream anymore. She said a big wedding was about a day, but loving each other was about a lifetime. And she had been so impatient! She was not about to wait until spring.

So, instead of a church and a dinner, instead of all those traditions she had once longed for, they had done as his grandmother had once done, and sent out a blanket invitation to spend Christmas with them. It had been like the days of old, the house filled to overflowing with joy and love. The wedding had been a surprise for most of their guests. A few, like Maggie, had been in on the secret.

So, after dinner, with only a few in the know, they had gone outside and lit a bonfire against the gathering darkness. Jefferson stood at the bonfire, down by the shores of the freshly frozen edges of the lake.

He still smiled with remembered delight as he

thought of the surprised faces of their friends and neighbors when Maggie's granddaughter had begun to play the wedding march on her flute. The notes had been so clear and beautiful on the crisp air that it had stunned their guests into silence. And then Pastor Michael had appeared, on cue, in his full vestments.

And then, the music had fallen away, and a pregnant sense of waiting had filled the gathering with a delightful sense of anticipation. Snow had fallen from the limb of a tree and landed with a poof of magic that had drawn all eyes there.

And there Angie had stood, at the edge of the old-growth forest, looking like an enchantment, looking every inch the angel he had always known she was, splendid in a white dress and a beautiful fur cape. Those curls had been sewn with tiny snowdrops, and she had come to him, through a path in the snow, her eyes never leaving his face, holding promises he could not have ever anticipated for himself.

They had spoken their vows on the shores of the lake, and now that spot was, forever, the most sacred of places. He could see it from where he stood at the window, now.

They had lit torches around the lake and strapped on skates, and that was where he had had the first dance with her. That year, the lake had frozen like glass, and they had been able to see the dark water far beneath them as they glided along. They had fire-roasted marshmallows instead of cake, and one of their friends had brought a guitar. They had sat by the fire singing and listening to the guitar and the flute dance with each other as the stars came out. He could not think of that day without his throat closing with pure emotion at how real every single moment of it had been.

Could it really have been three years this month? Sometimes he longed to stop the race of time, to hold each moment in his hand so that he could feel it more deeply, savor what he had been given.

He heard a shriek of laughter and grimaced good-naturedly. He turned back to what he was doing: painting this room a delicate shade of white that had the faintest blush of pink in it.

"It's the very same color," he had groused to Angie when she had shown it to him.

"No," she had said, "it's not," and so that had become the color of the nursery. He slid a little glance at the crib he had assembled yesterday and he gulped.

Were they ready for this? Could you ever be ready?

Angie had said to him once, on the most important day of his life, that there was no love without courage. She had said that to choose love, even though it wounded, was the greatest courage of all.

But in a month, they were going to have a baby in this room, in that crib with its bumpers and blankets with vivid pink monkeys cavorting across the fabric as if it was all fun, somehow. Fun? A real, live, breathing, cooing, little girl. He was not at all sure he had the courage for this.

Not just for bringing the baby home, but for the first day of kindergarten, and for wiping away tears because some boy had been mean to her, and for deciding whether she should be in hockey or ballet.

Was he ready to be a daddy? So much potential for love. And so much potential for loss. And so much potential for the place where those two things met.

Because even now, with his baby girl still safe in the womb of her mother, Jefferson ached with awareness.

That there would come a day, when she might want a long, dress of white or she might not, but there would come a day when she would stand in a place of sanctuary, looking at a man who was not her daddy, with an aching love in her eyes.

The laughter came again, floating up the staircases as if the house was overflowing with it.

Jefferson contemplated that. His house, once a lonely fortress on a rock, was filled with the sounds of his friends and neighbors, gathering from far and wide to celebrate Christmas here at the Stone House. It was remarkably easy to breathe new life into an old tradition. But then, really, Angie made so much look remarkably easy.

Angie had never returned to teaching home economics in high school. Instead, after they had married, she had started an organization called Prom-n-Aid.

She remembered, so clearly, being the child of a single parent, unable to afford what other girls could have. Trust Angie to turn this into her gift to the world. She proudly headed an organization that did not give girls dresses, but showed them how to create them.

"I don't just want to give them a dress," Angie had told him in that earnest way of hers. "I want them to discover the power of their own creativity—their ability to use the force of creativity to make the world match their dreams."

But really, for all those words, it was just a variation on love.

It had grown unbelievably. Angie taught seminars to teachers and clubs all over North America, showing them how to get sponsors to donate everything from thread to tiaras, how to reach out to the girls who needed this the most.

"There you are!"

Jefferson turned slightly. His wife—would he ever get accustomed to those words in relation to Angie—was glowing. For some reason, pregnancy had made her hair even curlier. How he loved the wild chaos of her hair. The maternity dress was of her own design, proudly hugging the huge roundness of her belly. She had been talking lately about starting a maternity division of Prom-n-Aid.

"It's beautiful," she whispered of the color.

"It's the same as it was before," he said, just for the sake of argument, even though he could clearly see it wasn't. The new shade had a delicacy and warmth that the old one had not had.

"Are you hiding?" she demanded, ignoring his invitation to argue with him, her eyes twinkling with the knowledge that she had his number.

"No. I just wanted to finish it, in case."

She did not accept his answer, watching him.

"Maybe," he admitted. "Maybe I'm hiding."

"Why?" she whispered.

He put his hand to his face and pinched his nose at the bridge, as if he could stop the emotion he was feeling. "I don't want everyone to see how scared I am to have this baby."

Angie came and tugged his hand away and looked at him in that way of hers that made him feel as if he was the strongest man in the universe.

And just like that, something flared between them, the something that never cooled or grew old. That allowed his wife to wrap him around her finger!

He carefully balanced the paintbrush on the open tin and left his hand in hers.

He heard the noises from downstairs again, and Maggie's laughter rose, joyous, above the others. She was so happy for him. They all were. It was as if he and Angie's love had become a part of the house, and it drew people here, into its circle. This is what love did.

It expanded. It gave back. It served.

It made the world better in ways that were too numerous to count, in ways that were as infinite as the stars in the sky.

Suddenly, he didn't feel afraid of having his own little girl at all.

Suddenly, he knew the biggest truth. His wife, his beautiful, wise, funny wife, could be wrong sometimes.

She had said, on the day she had come back for him, on the day she had refused to sacrifice him to the abyss of loneliness he would have chosen, that there was no love without courage. She had said to choose love, even when it wounded you, was the greatest courage of all.

But now, Jefferson saw a deeper truth.

It wasn't the *greatest* kind of courage, after all.

Choosing love was the *only* kind of courage.

"Are you ready?" Angie said.

She could have meant anything. Was he ready to join the others? Was he ready for Christmas dinner? Was he ready to welcome a baby into their lives?

"Yes," Jefferson said. He said it to the bigger question, the one that required the only kind of courage.

He said yes, again, just as he had three years ago, to the force that humbled a man completely, that was so much larger than anything he could ever be, that had plans for him that were so much bigger than anything he could have ever planned for himself. Jefferson Stone said yes to love.

* * * * *

MILLS & BOON®
Large Print – March 2016

A Christmas Vow of Seduction
Maisey Yates

Brazilian's Nine Months' Notice
Susan Stephens

The Sheikh's Christmas Conquest
Sharon Kendrick

Shackled to the Sheikh
Trish Morey

Unwrapping the Castelli Secret
Caitlin Crews

A Marriage Fit for a Sinner
Maya Blake

Larenzo's Christmas Baby
Kate Hewitt

His Lost-and-Found Bride
Scarlet Wilson

Housekeeper Under the Mistletoe
Cara Colter

Gift-Wrapped in Her Wedding Dress
Kandy Shepherd

The Prince's Christmas Vow
Jennifer Faye

MILLS & BOON®
Large Print – April 2016

The Price of His Redemption
Carol Marinelli

Back in the Brazilian's Bed
Susan Stephens

The Innocent's Sinful Craving
Sara Craven

Brunetti's Secret Son
Maya Blake

Talos Claims His Virgin
Michelle Smart

Destined for the Desert King
Kate Walker

Ravensdale's Defiant Captive
Melanie Milburne

The Best Man & The Wedding Planner
Teresa Carpenter

Proposal at the Winter Ball
Jessica Gilmore

Bodyguard...to Bridegroom?
Nikki Logan

Christmas Kisses with Her Boss
Nina Milne

MILLS & BOON®

Why shop at millsandboon.co.uk?

Each year, thousands of romance readers find their perfect read at millsandboon.co.uk. That's because we're passionate about bringing you the very best romantic fiction. Here are some of the advantages of shopping at www.millsandboon.co.uk:

* **Get new books first**—you'll be able to buy your favourite books one month before they hit the shops

* **Get exclusive discounts**—you'll also be able to buy our specially created monthly collections, with up to 50% off the RRP

* **Find your favourite authors**—latest news, interviews and new releases for all your favourite authors and series on our website, plus ideas for what to try next

* **Join in**—once you've bought your favourite books, don't forget to register with us to rate, review and join in the discussions

Visit **www.millsandboon.co.uk** for all this and more today!